The Path

Tales from a Revolution: Rhode-Island

D1312875

The Path

Lars D. H. Hedbor

Brief Candle
Press

Cover and book design: Brief Candle Press.
Cover image: Wilifred Ball, "A Path in the New Forest," 1906.
Map reproductions courtesy of Library of Congress, Geography and Map Division.
Fonts: Doves Type and IM FELL English.

First Brief Candle Press edition published 2017.
www.briefcandlepress.com

ISBN: 978-1-942319-24-5

Dedication

For Amy, Faye, Matt, Tammy, Diane, Andy,
Beatrice, Becky, Archie, Cassie, Laura, Jan, Keith,
Susy, Kristin, Cheryl, Lori, Alan, and Ken.

You know what you did.

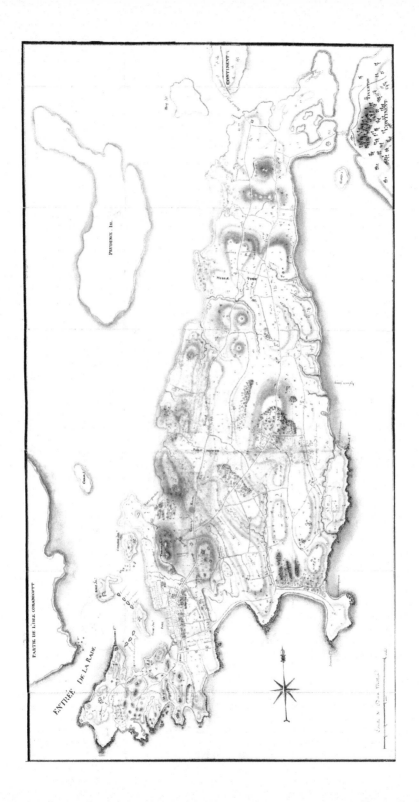

Chapter I

The springtime air was sweet, and the woods around Yves de Bourganes *dit Ledisciple*—his *nom de guerre* awarded in derision by a long-forgotten sergeant— fairly burst with the stirring of life reborn. His heart, however, was full of worry and doubt, and it was difficult for him to notice much about the beauty that surrounded him.

His *bas-officier* had woken him with the news that their company of *chausseurs* had received orders to march to Brest. There they were to embark upon a voyage over the sea to a destination unnamed, but widely expected to be either the shores of England, or the Indies, or even America itself. It was whispered that they might join in the battle against their perennial enemy, the English, by backing the rebellion of their colonies there.

Out of professional interest, of course, Yves had followed the news of events across the ocean. It seemed incredible that the colonists—who had mere years before taken part in an enthusiastic trouncing of French forces in America—might now become allies, never mind that they might actually stand a chance of winning their independence from Mother England.

However, a series of convincing victories against some of Britain's best armed divisions had made the unthinkable worth considering, and had recently spurred the French King to declare a formal alliance with the Americans, extending recognition of them as an independent nation of the Earth. Arms, cash, and even military forces had followed, but the war had dragged on without resolution, and the scuttlebutt around winter quarters was that France was preparing to redouble its commitment to bloodying King George's nose.

So, while Yves was not excited about being sent far away from family, neither was he surprised. The first flowers of spring, which he might have gathered into a garland for a girl's hair on another day, passed scarcely noticed, and instead his thoughts turned to home. There, where Yves had grown up, his mother struggled with the responsibilities of running a small farm in the wake of his father's death, and with raising his younger brothers.

His sister had married away just before his father's death, and was consumed with her own growing family. Yves had thought to relieve the burden on his mother by volunteering for the army, even though she had begged him not to, particularly with the new war stirring against Britain. Yves had assured her that the struggle would be concluded quickly—all the pamphlets circulated around town boasted of the superiority of the French forces over the British—but he had not honestly expected that he would wind up serving in that distant theater of war.

And yet here he was. Though their winter quarters were not very distant from his farm, Yves halfway wished that he could have delivered the news of his departure via letter, instead of feeling the obligation to face his mother personally. His step, though brisk out of military habit, was nonetheless reluctant, and he wished that the path were longer than it was, to give him more time to formulate a gentle way of telling his mother that he would be leaving within the week.

Alas, the fragrant whiff of woodland violets gave way too soon to the earthy smell of freshly-turned fields, and far sooner than he willed it, Yves stood before the door to the home where he had whiled away the hours of his boyhood. Then, his father had walked the Earth, and had managed the affairs of the farm with a stern but kindly manner. Meat and fish had graced their table more often than not, and his mother's smile had been generous and her laughter seemed like the music of house.

Now, as she opened the door to his knock, her smile was no less warm, but he could see the lines that graved the corners of her mouth and eyes, speaking of long nights of worry and seasons of grief. Her once auburn hair no longer glinted of fire in the sun, but was streaked with iron grey as it led to a tight bun on the back of her head.

She embraced him, saying, "Yves, I had not looked to see you again so soon, though I am overjoyed at your arrival." As she stepped back from him, she noted his expression, and added with a frown, "I can see already that you bring no happy tidings."

"*Maman*, I sail from Brest within the week. We are likely bound for Jamaica." Having failed to think of a gentle means of breaking the news, he had settled on a direct approach.

His mother's mouth set into a firm grimace, and she said only, "So? Come, have you supped?"

"You know that I would be derelict in my duties as a soldier and a son if I failed to enjoy a meal at your table whenever the opportunity presented itself."

Her grimace turned to a half-smile, and she said, "Well, then take off your boots and make yourself useful in the kitchen."

"Of course, *maman*." As he followed her into the house, he

permitted himself a small sigh of relief. He had worried that she would receive the news of his departure with greater visible upset; indeed, it seemed that she was even more resigned to it than he was.

In the kitchen, a pot bubbled gently over the fire, a fragrant meat broth, and Yves saw a bunch of carrots that his mother had left on the table, sitting beside several large potatoes. She bustled past him into the root cellar and emerged with several more of each. She handed him the vegetables and a knife saying only, "You know what needs to be done with these."

A small smile played around the corners of his mouth as he bent to the task. He knew, indeed, as he had spent many a tiresome hour in winter quarters peeling potatoes and scraping carrots. She might have tried to instruct him in the techniques, but he had perfected them in the service of the camp kitchens.

As he worked, she said suddenly, "How long will you spend in Jamaica?"

He shook his head, frowning. "I am not yet certain that Jamaica is even our destination. We might be bound instead for America or even further afield." He shrugged. "As for how long we may expect to be gone, I doubt that even those who send us are certain. If we sail for America, we may find useful employment there for some years of campaigning. If we are to be posted for routine guard duty someplace else, we may be back in mere months."

She looked at him sharply as he spoke of years of service in America, and frowned tightly again when he said the words "mere months."

"Do not think to quiet me with comfortable lies, Yves. You believe yourself to be bound for the American war, and I should

4

not expect to see you again in this life, with my advanced years and hard toil."

He sighed. "*Maman*, you have many years of health and vigor yet ahead of you, and the British Crown cannot sustain this war for much longer, if the reports from across the Channel are to be believed. King George bleeds the treasury white in the effort to retain his American colonies, and I've heard it said that Lord North has already submitted his resignation at least once, though the King refuses to accept it."

He smiled reassuringly. "If we are to join in the American war, it is even possible that we may strike the final blow that brings the British Army in North America to its knees, and ends this episode once and for all."

She glared at her son. "Again, you try to comfort me in my ignorance of martial matters, Yves. Even if this war should end, how long will it be before we are again called upon to take up arms against the English, and if not them, then the Spanish, or the Dutch, or the Swedish." She snorted. "The generals and the court at Versailles seem never to lack for cause to rattle swords and shed blood."

Tears sprang to her eyes and she wiped them away angrily, adding, "I only pray that the blood they shed shall not be yours, for what years that I am granted to live."

Yves sighed inwardly. This was exactly the sort of scene he had hoped to avoid with his mother, but he understood her worries, and even shared them. Life in the military had sounded like a good alternative to privation at the farm, until he had heard the stories of the older soldiers, men who had seen battle, and who told tales of the horrors of the cannonball and the bayonet . . . and the grisly results of disease, which carried off more than arms ever did.

"*Maman*, I have no choice in the matter at this point. I am sworn to follow the commands of my officers, and if they say I am to go to Jamaica, I will go to Jamaica. If I am to fight the redcoats, I will fight the redcoats. And"—he smiled—"if I am to peel potatoes, I will peel potatoes." With that, he pushed the bowl of potatoes, ready for the pot, across the table to her.

She gave him a grudging smile. "Well, at least you have learned something of use then." She took the bowl from him and said, "I only hope that you have learned as well how to stay out of the way of your enemy's bullets and sword, should you find yourself in the teeth of battle."

"I have paid close attention to what lessons in those skills have been offered to me, as I have only this one skin into which I was born, and I should like very much to keep it intact."

She fixed him with a piercing glare. "Mind that you do, Yves. I have buried a husband, and it nearly finished me. I do not expect that I could survive burying my eldest son as well."

"I understand, *maman*, and I will do all in my power to return to you whole and unhurt."

She nodded crisply and put the vegetables into the pot, saying over her shoulder, "Call your brothers in from the fields. By the time they are clean enough to sit at the table, this will be ready."

Chapter 2

"Eat while you can, my friend." Yves looked up to see Luc, his long-time companion in the company, approaching the table where he was breaking fast with a fish stew, accompanied by half a loaf of bread.

Luc eased into the seat beside Yves, setting down a plate heavily laden with the same stew, and a whole loaf of bread besides. "In just a few days, you'll be glad to be able to choke down a dry crust of bread—or worse, ship's biscuit. By the time we reach our destination, you'll be able to feel your ribs through your uniform." He smiled slyly, adding, "Unless you're one of the blessed few who are fortunate enough to be possessed of an iron stomach, immune to the action of the waves and wind."

Yves rolled his eyes and returned to his meal. "Sometimes, Luc, I think that you make things up just to justify eating an extra portion when it suits you."

Luc shrugged. "Suit yourself. You'll learn by experience soon enough."

Yves retorted, "I have been in a boat before, and suffered no ill effect."

"Ah, but have you been on a ship of war in the open ocean, with the horrid smells of your fellow soldiers pressing close upon you, even as your whole world moves wildly around you, seemingly without cause or reason?" Luc dug Yves in the ribs, saying, "Once you have weathered that and eaten hearty, then you should come and speak to me again."

Yves said nothing, but reflected that his friend was more likely than not to be right, as he did have the experience of a posting to the West Indies under his belt—and this would be Yves' first true ocean voyage.

"Are the rations shipboard really as bad as you say?"

"Worse, my friend, than you can believe. Oh, the officers eat decently, but the soldiers' mess is confined only to those items which will store well in a barrel for month after month, and which the soldiers will eat even if they are spoiled by damp or age."

"Have the cooks no interest in ensuring that we arrive ready to perform what duties are to be asked of us at our destination?"

"So long as they deliver us alive, they consider that their duty is complete." Yves made a sour face in reply, and Luc laughed. "So now you understand why I am working so hard to prepare for the rigors of our voyage."

Yves snorted and said, "If by 'working,' you mean exactly the opposite of what the word means, perhaps."

"Well, then you have understood me perfectly, Yves." Luc winked and grinned, turning back to his food. "Best you finish what is before you, and see if you can beg a second serving, eh?"

Yves said nothing, but addressed his meal with renewed interest and appreciation. Even if the food were so awful as Luc claimed, Yves felt pretty sure that he had eaten more poorly in the lean months on the farm before he had joined the army, and he was confident in his ability to weather any privation that the voyage might bring him.

Luc changed the subject abruptly, asking, "What have you

heard of the Americans and their military order?"

Yves shrugged noncommittally. "They are led by men trained in the English manner of things, though it seems that they are open to learning better ways from our officers."

Luc nodded. "I have heard much the same, though I spoke to one officer who was admiring of their creativity and agility on the battlefield. Too, it seems that they have surprised our English friends many times by using tactics that are, to be blunt, downright uncivilized."

Yves frowned in reply. "The English have conducted themselves in uncivil manner on occasion as well, if the reports are to be believed."

"War is no civilized matter, under any conditions, but a war that pits a nation against itself is liable to be the most savage of all." Luc shuddered. "I do not envy our English neighbors, nor their American cousins, their war, and I only wish that King Louis had found a way to keep us clear of it."

Yves looked around to see if anyone were in earshot. "You should be careful in giving voice to thoughts critical of the King. One never knows when you might be misunderstood to lack in fealty to our sovereign."

Luc grimaced and nodded. "I mean only that it seems to be that it would have been advantageous to our nation to have stood back and let them weaken one another, even without our help."

"That's a fair thought, though from what I've heard, the war would have been long over, with the English ascendant, had we stayed our hand and withheld our assistance to the American cause. So, perhaps the King and his advisors are cleverer than you grant them credit for, and have used the forces at their disposal to prolong the conflict, to the advantage that you imagined."

Luc pursed his mouth thoughtfully, then nodded slowly. "I suppose that it is possible that they are playing a cannier game than I had thought." He took another bite of stew and chewed it thoughtfully, then shrugged. "In any case, I mean to eat heartily while there is yet edible food before me, and solid ground on which to sleep."

Yves stuffed the last of his bread into his mouth and nodded, rising to return to the canteen. Luc waved cheerily to him, and tore off another chunk of bread to fill his own mouth.

Yves' legs were still sore from the march to the docks at Brest, and he walked slowly to the canteen. It wasn't that he was unused to walking distances, but marching in good order for a day and a half, with scarcely a pause to attend to the demands of nature, was never easy.

He supposed, though, that he would do well to accustom himself to such rigors against the possibility of service in America itself, for the one constant he had heard from everyone who had spent any time there was that it was a huge, untamed country, and movements from one city to another were strenuous and lengthy affairs. It was fraught, too, with the added danger of both English units, and the less-civilized American Loyalist rabble and their downright savage Indian allies.

Yves did not believe most of the stories told around the campfire at night about the feats accomplished by the Indians in battle—more reasoned voices pointed out that they were but human, and not beings of myth. However, the haunted look in the eyes of some he had heard from gave credence to the savagery of their stories. Still—cutting the scalp off of an enemy's head to keep as a trophy, or trussing a man to a tree and burning him alive? This was a level of inhumanity that he found difficult to countenance.

As for the Indies, most of what he had heard about service there revolved around heat, vicious insects, and lurid tales of the diseases that lurked in its swamps. He tried to reassure himself, though, that the stories of either possible posting were of the same nature as the tales his siblings had told him around the hearth late at night, designed for their own satisfaction at seeing him squirm in discomfort.

His musings were interrupted by the call of an officer, loud enough to be heard over the general hubbub of the canteen. "All units, come to order immediately! We are commanded to board at once, in preparation for our departure. *Toute de suite!*"

Yves was as startled as those around him appeared to be, but he hurried back to where his campmates were already busy striking camp, pulling stakes out of the ground and rolling canvas. He joined in, seizing a corner of the tent and holding it steady while another man lifted the opposite corner and walked it over to him.

Their movements were practiced and unhurried, but in a matter less than an hour, all that remained of a campsite that had housed hundreds of men were the smoldering pits from a couple of poorly-extinguished fires; the rest was packed away in haversacks and trunks, dry and ready for reassembly wherever their voyage might take them.

The men stood in regular lines, as though prepared for inspection, though their uniforms would not have withstood a full examination. Their effects, however, were carefully stacked, and the company clerk was moving down the line with a jar of black paint and a brush, quickly and carefully labeling each barrel and trunk that was not yet marked, and refreshing the labels on those that were.

Beside Yves, Luc stood at an approximation of attention, and Yves couldn't help but notice that the other man's haversack bulged strangely. Luc saw him staring and leaned over to whisper, "Grabbed another few loaves of bread in the confusion. We'll likely not board by end of day, and then you'll be glad I am willing to share."

Yves smiled at his friend, and was about to reply when he heard the familiar regular, firm step of their company adjutant coming up behind them along the line, and both soldiers drew themselves up to attention. The *bas-officier* walked past, nodding in approval at the ranks as he went.

The man stopped at the head of the company where their captain waited and together the two looked them over for a few moments. Finally, he nodded to the captain, who then spoke. "Men, you will board behind your sergeants, and pay close heed to the instructions given you by the sailors on board your ships. Our company will sail aboard a privateer hired by the Navy to provide for our passage. She is *Baron D'Arras*, and I am assured that she is both seaworthy and as comfortable as can be expected."

He paused for a moment, again regarding the company with a clear mixture of approval and confidence. When he spoke again, it was louder and clearer than before, and with a sense of joy and pride. "We sail under the command of le Compte de Rochambeau, who has agreed to lead an *Expédition Particulière* to aid our new allies, these United States of America, to complete the task of breaking the colonies in North America free of the British King once and for all. Let us go forth for victory and honor!"

The adjutant grinned as the captain turned and departed. "All right, you heard the captain. Form up and follow me. We board at once."

Chapter 3

They may have boarded at once, but that did not mean that they departed with as much haste. First, they had to find their way belowdecks, where the only light was what filtered through the hatches and a few small lanterns, wholly inadequate in the gloom.

Closely-spaced hammocks were assigned to paired-off soldiers—Yves and Luc, naturally, contrived to share one—and they were instructed that they would take turns sleeping in them. In practice, Luc informed Yves, one man usually slept on the filth-encrusted deck, while the other slept in the relative comfort of the hammock.

Even in the first moments as he descended into the darkness, Yves' nose rebelled at the ancient stench of men who had not washed since any accounting, mingled with the smells produced by frightened and overcrowded livestock, spoiled food, and bilge water below that defied classification beyond simply "hellish."

Their haversacks stored beneath their hammock, Yves and Luc went to look at the rest of the ship. Of course, all of the other landsmen freshly aboard were trying to do likewise, while the sailors were striving to load provisions and otherwise make ready for departure.

One sailor spotted the pair emerging into the sunlight onto the deck, and called out, "You two! With me, to help shift barrels in the hold."

Luc cursed under his breath, and Yves scowled and drew breath to protest, but Luc elbowed him in the ribs. He whispered harshly, "We must do as he says, else face the captain's lash."

Yves followed his friend, but whispered back, "Would our captain truly resort to the lash over such a trifle?"

Luc shot him a pitying look. "Our captain might or might not . . . but *his* captain would relish the chance to make an example of two of his human cargo."

Yves' eyes widened as he comprehended what Luc was getting at, and he quickened his step to keep up with the sailor.

Some hours later, both men had seen every corner of the foul tub that would be their home for the coming months of their voyage, but both could scarcely move for exhaustion. As he collapsed under their hammock—Luc had won the toss for it—Yves had a better appreciation for the sources of each of the aromas that still assailed them.

While some of the endless barrels he and Luc had rolled from one place to another in the dank hold had borne the markings of their company, others had clearly been down there for months already, their staves stained by the damp. Some of the supplies they had moved needed to be crammed into mostly-dry spaces above the bilge, though there was no way to access those spaces but to splash through ankle-deep liquid.

Yves shuddered at the memory, and could smell the particular aroma of that polluted water from Luc's shoes where they lay just above his nose, even amongst the competing smells of the close belowdecks space. He lacked the energy to do more, though, and was asleep before he could finish a thought about how to avoid such service in the future.

He awoke to a clamor of bells and feet stomping about wildly on the deck overhead. Inches over his face, Luc shifted in the hammock, and a drop of something splashed onto Yves' cheek from the other man's feet. That was enough to rouse him from his cramped position on the hard floor, and he scrambled out from under the hammock with a variety of unkind words on his lips for Luc.

His friend's face in repose, however, was so angelic that the incongruence with their surroundings made him laugh aloud. "Come, my friend," he said to Luc, jostling the other man's shoulder to wake him. "Let us see what the commotion above is."

Luc opened his eyes to a slit and cocked his head, listening for a moment before he answered. "It's only the changing of the watch. We have two more bells of rest yet before we need worry ourselves about making an appearance for our meal." He closed his eyes again and relaxed back into the hammock.

Yves regarded his friend suspiciously. "How can you know all that from listening to the clomp of boots on the deck for a moment?"

Luc opened his eyes again and grunted, "Heard the bells before you got up, so I knew what watch it was. You'll learn, too, in time. Meanwhile, grab some deck for a while longer and make the most of the time we're permitted to sleep." His eyes closed again, and he rolled to face away.

Yves frowned at his friend's back for a moment, and then lowered himself back to the deck, where he laid down with his head at the same end as Luc's this time. As he began to drift off to sleep, Luc's raucous snoring began, and it took several minutes longer for

Yves to actually return to unconsciousness.

He awoke screaming, as *something* scurried across his face. The tail of a very large rat disappeared into a hole where the sloping hull met the deck, and Yves practically levitated out from under the hammock. Luc stirred and rolled again to face him.

He sighed at Yves, whose heart was still hammering in his chest. He asked wearily, "What is it now, Yves?"

Yves shuddered and answered, "It was a rat, crossing my face as I slept. It escaped through a hole down there." He gestured at the spot where he had last seen the creature.

Luc looked over the side of the hammock with apparent interest. "Fat one?"

"It looked as though it has eaten well of late, yes."

Luc nodded sagely. "Good, good. We'll have to set a snare and catch it before these other fellows do, then." Seeing Yves' confusion, he laughed. "Rats are good eating, far better than the slop the cook will sling. It's a stroke of good fortune that we have found one so early in the voyage. Where there is one, there will be more, and we'll eat well for a piece, as a result."

He grinned at Yves' expression of abject distaste. "After you've had nothing but grog and slop for a week, you'll change your tune, I'll wager." He shrugged, adding with another grin, "And, if not, more for me."

At that moment, the bell rang and again there was the rush of footfalls overhead. Luc swung his feet over the side of the hammock, stretched and rubbed a knot out of his back, and said, "Let us go and test that theory now, shall we? It's mealtime."

Yves was accustomed to unrefined manners, growing up with younger brothers, even under the determined guidance of their mother. His time so far in the army had further inured him to the hazards of sharing a table with men of widely-varying social status and breeding.

However, he found that even he was shocked at the crude language, casual rudeness, and flatly disgusting table habits of the sailors who manned their transport. He had heard tales—many from Luc—of civilized and convivial tables aboard naval vessels, but either those stories were wildly exaggerated, or the same standards did not obtain amongst the crew of a mere privateer.

As for the food, the pork-flavored porridge wasn't quite so bad as Luc had described, though it was not nearly as good as Yves had grown accustomed to. In any event, Yves could remember many nights after his father's death when all that was available to fill their bellies was a thin gruel of a handful of oats and perhaps some wilted cabbage that should really have gone to the chickens.

As he grew accustomed to the shocking lack of table graces among his dining companions, Yves surreptitiously examined their appearance. Their clothing was rough but sturdy, consisting of coarsely-woven, undyed or black cloth, which consistently appeared to have been sewn by someone who was more accustomed to the rugged construction of sails than the seams of clothing.

Their faces were as filthy as the bilge, and it appeared that between the lot of them, they owned but one dull razor. Their eyes, though, were lively and, for the most part, promised intelligence. Unfortunately, that intelligence seemed at the moment to be mostly applied to the problem of how best to make the landsmen uncomfortable.

"Ah, I cannot wait until we reach the open sea," said one, an evil twinkle in his eye. "No land in sight, and nothing to warn of a gale to come. You remember, Karl, the 'urrican we encountered off the Indies—what?—three years back?"

The one who was presumably named Karl, nodded and grunted. No intelligence lit his eyes, but his shoulders bulged with ropy muscle, a quality that Yves guessed compensated adequately for his sparkling mealtime conversational skills.

"Snapped the main and mizzen right off, it did, and would have sent us to the bottom, if you hadn't been there to clear the wreckage and let us float free."

Karl grunted again and gave his full attention to his meal. If Yves had thought the brute capable of the emotion, he would have sworn that Karl was embarrassed at what was clearly a relished retelling of an old sea tale.

"I thought we were finished, though, when the kraken arose at the height of the storm and seized you up in its slimy tentacles and waved you about until you could find your knife and give it reason to drop you back onto the deck." The man's eyes jumped over to Luc, to see whether he was paying attention. Luc gave him a tired half smile and silently shook his head.

Yves feigned boredom in emulation of his friend, but a piece of him couldn't help but wonder whether a beast swam the seas capable of lifting the powerful Karl overhead in the teeth of a raging tempest. The storyteller snorted in disgust, and Karl rose to leave the table, giving Yves and Luc what appeared to be an apologetic look as he went.

Chapter 4

The routine of shipboard life became monotonous within a day or two of their boarding, and all the more so for the fact that they remained rocking at anchor in the harbor at Brest. Yves diverted himself for a while standing at the railing, looking out at the activity surrounding the great fleet that was gathering.

The bay was immense, with the docks and the walls of the town rising behind them at one end, and villages visible all along its shores. An exceptional number of ships lay at anchor all about the bay. While nearly fifty vessels were preparing for the voyage to America, countless other ships, ranging from waddling merchants to enormous Navy ships of the line, could be seen taking on cargo, conducting maintenance, or simply sitting and waiting for a favorable tide and wind.

Yves quickly learned not to be spotted idle, lest he be pressed into some labor that not even the sailors wished to do. Not that there was a lot that they weren't willing to do. Much as it pained him to admit it, the crew of the privateer worked harder and more intensely than any human beings he had ever observed at close quarters.

When the bell for their watch sounded, they sprang from their hammocks as though the devil himself drove them—and having seen the scars that some bore on their backs of vicious floggings endured for some past infraction, Yves could well understand why. Nor was the whip spared even here at anchor, on calm water. More than once, Yves heard the whistle and crack of a man being disciplined, invariably answered with silence and clamped jaws.

For all of the petty violence of their discipline, Yves did not see how the ever-present threat of physical assault improved the quality of the sailors' work, though he could not deny that its speed was unmatched.

The prevailing philosophy seemed to be that it was better to do something wrong and await correction than to ask for clarification and receive the whip. Sloppy work was the rule, not the exception, and it was clear that many of the crew shared only a few words in a common tongue with the officers or the soldiers of the company. Communication was haphazard at best, and shouting matches were the most frequent means employed to attempt to overcome the barriers of language and temperament.

The officers of the privateer did not whip or even shout much at members of the company, of course. They did press the soldiers into labor whenever possible, and there was no lack of tasks that had to be done on a constant, routine basis. Yves could only guess how much more strenuous the daily cycle of work would become once they set out to sea.

And then, one morning, they did raise anchor. The crew of the privateer seemed to be working more or less in concert now, though even a landsman's eye could see the contrast between the indifferent manner in which their ship's sails were shaken out and the crisp, nearly instantaneous appearance of the sails of the Navy's ships in the fleet.

On another privateer nearby, though, even greater chaos

clearly reigned, and Yves heard shouts of alarm from others on the deck that alerted him to look up in time to see the ship actually collide headlong into the side of one of the great naval vessels. The two ships shuddered to a halt, bound together by tangled debris and cordage.

Even from a distance of several times his own ship's length, Yves could hear the stream of shouted abuse that erupted from the Navy ship, directed at the men on the deck of the much smaller privateer. It was mingled with the coarse shouts of the ordinary sailors on both vessels as they sprang to clear the wreckage and free the two ships from one another.

The smaller ship swung around on a hastily-dropped anchor and pulled away from the warship, accompanied by the splashes of pieces of debris raining down onto the water. A small mast of some sort with a sail still bound to it was the largest piece, but various splintered pieces of wood and gear also splashed into the harbor.

A crowd gathered on the railing of their own ship, consisting mostly of landsmen, though off-watch sailors stood transfixed as well. Sailors on duty split their attention between the drama unfolding off the left—or, as Yves was learning to call it, the "port"—bow, and attending to their duties to avoid creating another such spectacle themselves.

Yves could see that the sail and rigging that emerged from the bow of the privateer had actually gone into the galley of the larger ship, smashing the carved image of a woman that had adorned the front of the privateer.

As the two ships parted farther, the damage to the warship was revealed to be nearly inconsequential, though the naval cook could be seen through the splintered hatch of the galley, sadly surveying the jumbled condition of his workplace. A copper kettle nearly large enough for a man to bathe in was crushed beyond repair, and he could be seen shoving it through the hole in the galley wall, to splash into the water of the harbor.

Aboard the damaged privateer, officers of both the ship's company and the regiment it was to carry stood clustered around the mangled prow of the ship. Already, a launch from the docks was being pulled swiftly by oarsmen to examine the privateer, and the naval warship was moving away from the scene of the collision to join the line of the fleet.

The captain of their own ship had had enough of the spectacle himself, and shouted for everyone to return to their assigned tasks at once, that they might likewise take their place in the convoy as it formed up to leave the harbor. Yves nevertheless snuck glances at the damaged privateer as it was towed back to the docks for repairs. He wondered if the ship, and the forces aboard it, would even be able to rejoin the expedition, or if the Compte's plans had already suffered their first abrupt change.

The convoy sailed away, leaving its damaged member behind, and lined up neatly to sail through the narrow passage at the mouth of the bay. All along the way, small craft accompanied them, with local citizens, merchants, wives, girlfriends, and less formal companions all shouting farewells and good wishes to the men aboard the ships.

By nightfall, the fleet was within sight of the open Atlantic Ocean, and anchored in close order under the watchful cannon of a fortress built high atop a tiny island just offshore of the coast.

All night, though, the ship was tossed by choppy, unpleasant seas, and Yves began to wonder whether Luc's advice had been more sensible than he had believed. He wasn't alone, as nearly all of the landsmen spent much of the night along the railing of the ship instead of grabbing what rest they could belowdecks.

The next morning, the privateer's crew were in foul moods, and when Luc finally dared to ask one what the cause was, the man growled, "The wind blows from an unfavorable quarter, and so we are to return to port until it shifts. This was all a waste of effort and time that we could have spent in the comfortable shelter of the bay. Somebody was in too great a hurry to be bothered with checking the weather."

He'd turned abruptly to return to his duties then, and Luc turned to Yves with an expressive shrug. "Perhaps, with luck, we'll be granted leave to venture ashore one last time while we wait, that we might remind ourselves again why we fight." He raised his eyebrows suggestively, and laughed at Yves' scowl.

Yves shook his head at his friend, saying only, "Not everything revolves around such pursuits, my friend."

Luc gave him a reproachful smile and said simply, "Perhaps not. But I am willing to take that risk."

It was not to be, however. The fleet anchored again at the port—rejoined by the hastily-repaired privateer that had suffered the collision—and then stood at alert, ready to leave the moment that the tide and wind indicated.

A fortnight after their first abortive attempt at departure, the signal went out early in the morning, and the fleet again weighed anchor. As before, the ships gathered in neat formation, the privateers' stationkeeping much improved for two weeks' attention to training and drill. None wanted to repeat the embarrassment suffered in the first attempt at departure.

As the Sun rose behind them, the fleet sailed out of the harbor again, the seas smooth and the winds favorable. It sailed without pause past its earlier anchorage at the fortress, and continued through the breakers at the mouth of the bay, into the Atlantic, and out of view of the land.

By the end of the day, the fleet stretched out prettily along an otherwise empty ocean, the sails of the ships in front of them lit from behind by the Sun lying low to the horizon off the bow of the ship. After the evening meal and grog, Yves stood for a moment at the railing of the ship, gazing into the sunset and contemplating the land that lay beyond that far horizon. The next shore he would see would be that of their destination, come what may.

Chapter 5

It was several days before anything broke the monotony of rising with the bells, performing whatever menial tasks the crew asked of them, eating food that grew increasingly unpalatable, and taking either the hammock or the deck underneath to sleep, as well as the consistently foul weather and rolling waves would permit.

Yves had grown inured to the constant press of other passengers close by, and scarcely noticed the stench that had threatened to unman him when first he boarded the tub. He supposed that the open air of the untrammeled ocean helped to carry off the worst of it, and the crews periodically laboring over the pumps had driven overboard the wretched bilge.

Manning the pumps was one of the tasks that the crew of the privateer felt that the landsmen could be trusted to do without constant supervision and exhortations. A few hours on the pump handle convinced Yves that pumping a bilge was a task invented specifically for the purpose of giving incentive to learn some more useful shipboard skill, so that one could no longer be spared for the mindless toil.

Yves' supposition that the bilge had been emptied was supported by the fact that they only needed to run the pumps for an hour or two every few days. However, the theory suffered a fatal blow when a trip to retrieve a smallish barrel squirreled away deep belowdecks proved that the water in the bilge was far from fresh—indeed, if anything it smelled worse than it had when the company had boarded.

The sailor who had deputized Yves to assist at the task of retrieving the barrel wrinkled his nose as they opened the hatch to the bilge, but then nodded approvingly.

"Bilge still smells like a tight, happy ship," he remarked. "As the saying goes, a sweet bilge portends a sour ship." Yves shot the man a puzzled look over the forearm he held pressed against his nose to block as much of the overpowering aroma as possible.

"Means that the ship don't leak much," the sailor said. "Ship leaks too much, she founders and sinks, and isn't much good to anyone except the fish. We air-breathers like a ship what holds her water nicely, you follow?"

Yves nodded, eager to end the lesson and return to someplace further removed from the hold, as he was beginning to feel faint, and the end of the barrel he held was in danger of slipping from his grip and into the bilge water.

Just then, they heard a cry being passed above from one person to another—"Sail!" "The *Amazone* has sighted a sail!"

The crewman gave Yves a broad grin and lifted his end of the barrel, saying, "Come, we don't want to miss the show! It's not every day you get to see a frigate go about its true work."

After they delivered the barrel to the officer who'd requested it—it turned out to be packed with preserved oranges from Portugal, and both men received a fruit for their troubles—they found their way to the deck.

While a cluster of crewmen and soldiers stood at the starboard railing looking out, both the frigate and her quarry were already below the horizon. Yves found Luc standing among the other men and gave him a questioning look.

Luc shrugged. "The signals said that she was giving chase to a ship bound for the East, but she turned out to be Swedish, and so neutral in this war." He turned away from the railing, and Yves noticed for the first time that his friend was looking gaunt and pale.

He said sharply, "Luc, are you unwell?"

Luc nodded, looking wan. "My stomach has forgotten all that it learned on the last voyage about withstanding the rigors of travel." He shrugged. "Once we get out of the great Bay of Gascony and into the open ocean, perhaps I will stop counting shirts."

Yves gave him a puzzled look, and Luc laughed weakly. "It's what the sailors say that one is doing at the rail in bad seas."

"Ah. Have you seen the ship's surgeon?"

"Why should I bother him over a simple case of *mal de mer*? The cure is to find a smoother sea, and the fleet strives daily for that goal already." He reached out and slapped Yves on the shoulder. "Worry not on my account, but take care of yourself."

Yves smiled briefly and replied, "I've only suffered when the storms rise while I am belowdecks. Out in the fresh air, I fare better."

"You have the luck of a first-time traveler then, my friend. I pray that it does not abandon you."

One of the crewmen emerged from the hatch and called out, "You, there. Come and help me re-wrap this line." Yves gave his friend a friendly return of his slap on the shoulder and followed the sailor forward.

A few days later, the fleet sailed on under low clouds but gentle seas, the light of midday filtering through the grey that dominated the skies. The Swedes had evaded *Amazone*, and she had resumed her station in the convoy.

Someone told Yves that one of the ships had sighted land as they passed by Spain's Cape Ortégal, but he saw nothing to port, where it might have been visible. The rolling chop that had so far plagued the fleet dissipated, and it seemed to Yves that the conditions could hardly be more ideal for putting the leagues behind them, so as to return to *terra firma* as quickly as possible.

However, the crewmen of the privateer seemed on edge, and he noticed more than one examining the horizon to starboard. Finally, his curiosity overcame him, and he approached a sailor he'd sat to eat with on several occasions now, a weather-beaten old soul who went by the odd moniker "Fid."

"What do the crew look for to starboard?"

Fid gave him a long, inscrutable look. "The sky is warning us," he said finally. "These seas are more rough than they ought be, as though a terrible squall has recently passed through." He frowned, his lower lip sagging to reveal a gap in his teeth where one had fallen out. "A place that has had one such storm may soon spawn another. On our last voyage, we were nearly dashed on the rocks on just a day such as this. Is it any wonder that some of us are watchful?"

"No, that sounds prudent. But cannot this ship weather a squall without difficulty, so long as the rocks are kept at a safe distance?"

"Yes, and we are far from any such hazards . . . but close by other ships of the convoy, and I'd almost rather run aground than face the wrath of another captain whose ship has been hurt by our inattention or back luck." He motioned around to the crewmen on deck. "About half of these men are new, and prone to making mistakes when we need to be executing orders as one."

He shrugged. "We who have been aboard *d'Arras* for some time have reason for our nerves, but it is more likely than not that we worry without cause."

Their worry was not without cause, but their concern was misplaced. The squall they feared struck at the front of the convoy, doing some little damage and slowing the faster ships. For once, the signal flags did not scold the privateer to make more sail to keep up with the rest.

Another squall struck entirely without warning the following night, waking Yves from a comfortable sleep and pleasant dreams. The wind and waves carried off some of the rigging, and one soldier who had been seen sick at the railing was nowhere to be found on board.

The ship's captain included the man by name in the Sunday prayers the next morning, but that was the extent of the observation that a human life had been snuffed out by the sea. Yves thought that this lack of regard for the value of a man spoke volumes to the question of the company's place on the ship. They were tolerated pests, but hardly worth memorializing in the end.

Contrary to his claims, Luc did not improve as they reached more steady seas, and on rising from under their hammock a few days later, Yves found his friend too weak to climb out and join the men on the deck. He asked another soldier to help him to lift Luc, and together they carried the man into the fresh air. Yves hurried to the galley and returned with food for his friend.

Luc sat with his back against the side of the quarterdeck, his face slack and grey, and only his eyes showing a spark of life. Yves sat by his side, concern etched into his face, and spooned the morning gruel into his friend's mouth.

Between labored bites, Luc spoke suddenly. "My girl at Penmeur, she informed me just before we left that she will bear me a child. She begged me to marry, but I told her that a mere soldier cannot afford a wife and child." He paused to breathe with effort. "I had hoped to share in some spoils on this expedition, and to make enough of my fortune to return to her."

He shook his head ruefully and grabbed Yves' arm with a surprisingly strong grip. Luc's eyes took on a sudden intense fire as he held his friend's gaze fiercely. "When you get home, look for Marie-Thérèse le Gare, and just tell her that I meant to¬—"

His hand on Yves' arm suddenly tightened in a spasm, and his eyes rolled back. Yves looked around desperately and called out to a passing sailor, "Fetch the surgeon! My friend, he is ill!"

He felt Luc's grip on him loosen, and he turned back to see his companion slump to the deck, his eyes open but unseeing, and his gaunt chest no longer stirring with breath.

The surgeon puffed up from belowdecks, but slowed his step as he took in the scene of Yves cradling his friend's corpse in his lap, tears coursing down his cheeks. The doctor sighed and turned away to look for the tailor. A length of sailcloth, weighted with ballast rock, was the only thing he could now offer for the second victim of the rigors of the voyage.

Chapter 6

The next few days passed without much of anything drawing Yves' lasting attention. He rose, he ate, he worked, and he slept. After Luc's body slid over the rail of the ship, with her captain standing by with his Bible to say a few perfunctory words before returning to his duties, nothing else seemed worth focusing on.

He'd known Luc since the first days of his service with the company. As Yves had stumbled through drill, Luc had been the one who taken the time to explain to him where his mistakes were, while the *bas-officiers* tended to rely on simply increasing the volume and pace of their instructions.

While he didn't consciously consider Luc a substitute for his lost father, Yves had found that he could go to his friend with any question, and whether or not Luc knew the answer, he at least had an opinion that he was glad enough to share. Most of those opinions had involved unlikely configurations of his least favorite *bas-officiers*, sometimes together with miscellaneous farm implements.

A few weeks before they had departed on this accursed expedition, Yves had asked him why he had not sought a promotion to *bas-officier* himself, and that was one of the few questions that Luc hadn't answered immediately. He'd shrugged and turned away, and Yves supposed that the conversation was concluded.

However, a few minutes later, Luc had turned back and said soberly, "Perhaps, in time, my friend. It may even be that this time approaches more quickly than we think. I cannot afford to purchase such a promotion—if my family were wealthy, I would have simply bought a commission and been done with it—but in battle, one can sometimes rise to an earned level of competence without the intercession of a financial transaction."

Yves remembered the wistful look in his friend's eye as he'd replied, and wondered whether Luc might have recently gotten the news from Marie-Thérèse, and whether the thought of how to provide for her and his child had been weighing heavily on his mind already.

Yves had no idea how he might pursue the fulfillment of Luc's dying wish. As he performed another menial task, his mind worried at the problem like a cat at a loose string. If fortune should return him to France, if he remained attached to the company—his term of enlistment would expire within a few months of the end of this voyage—if he happened to return to the same winter quarters.

He shook his head angrily. And even if he could find the girl, what was he to do for her and her child? He was no more situated to provide meaningful support than Luc had been, and even if he had been, how could he meet the obligation to another man's bastard child? Nothing he could even contemplate would offer the baby legitimacy, and that assumed that the girl—and Yves himself—were even willing to make some form of a marriage.

He sighed. The mood of those around him was little better than his own. Their ship had slipped to the tail end of the convoy, and those ships ahead were having to stop and wait for her to catch up almost daily. Yves heard mutterings among the crewmen that the captain had been remonstrated via signal flag, in full view of the whole fleet, and essentially accused of being too shy of the danger posed by pressing every sail he possessed into service, that his ship might keep pace.

The masts sprouted more sails, but the wallowing tub still trailed behind the convoy daily. There was a real danger in what might have been merely an embarrassment—should an enemy ship approach the convoy from the rear, her distance from the warships, combined with the fact that she was laden with fighting men, made her a ripe target for attack.

When the day came that the cry of "Sail! Sail on the horizon!" went up, Yves could feel the tension rise so much that even in his distant and distracted state, he shared in it to some degree. He peered, along with the others, to starboard where the sails of two ships could now be perceived. When they drew closer to the fleet, an officer on one of the warships was able to make out in his glass that they flew the flag of Sweden again.

Fid happened to be standing nearby when the word spread along the rail where Yves stood, and Yves heard him say under his breath, "I wish that they would either take a part or else leave us in peace, but in either case, stop causing us alarm." He followed his comment with a gob of spit over the rail and went back to his work.

Shortly afterward, the Swedes drew away, clearly satisfied in their own curiosity as to the identity of the great expedition against which they had brushed. The tension about the ship dropped palpably as their sails were lost beneath the horizon. Ships flying false colors had fooled better captains than theirs.

Over the next few days, more sails appeared on the horizon

to port, but they never drew close enough for even the frigates to give chase, disappearing back under the edge of the sea as quickly as they had appeared.

More days passed, and the commander of the expedition continued to express his displeasure with the little transport. Finally, in resignation, he signaled for a faster transport to attach towlines to the *Baron d'Arras*, to enable her to stay within safe distance of the fleet.

If the crewmembers' mood had been dour before, it was downright murderous now. They took it as a personal insult that their ship, creaky and slow though she might be, would now be dragged through the ocean behind a faster ship, like a child pulling a toy.

The ship's master kept after them to make sail, so as to try to make the towline go slack, thus proving its redundancy, but the sad fact of the matter was that there was one slowest ship in any fleet—and the *Baron* was this expedition's sad case.

Yves stood at the starboard rail a couple of days after the towline had been emplaced, looking toward where the Sun lay low on the horizon, casting long shadows behind him. The sea air was warm and salty, and the towline pulled the privateer across the waves awkwardly, so that waves slapped into the side of the ship, regularly raising spray up to the railing.

While he knew that his clothes would be stiff and uncomfortable after they dried, the spray cooled Yves' skin, and he considered the exchange a fair one. The sound of a splash at the bow made him whip his head around as he looked to see whether another man had fallen overboard.

He could see no human form in the water, but there was

something there, and he gave a sigh of relief as he made out some sort of enormous fish swimming alongside the prow of the ship. A second and a third joined the first, and then one of them leapt up out of the water, producing another alarming explosion of spray, carried back to where Yves stood.

The three fish cavorted for a long while in the bow-wave of the ship, and Yves was joined at the railing by Fid. The sailor watched for a moment, and then said, "Dolphin. Hard as hell to catch, but I hear tales that they are not bad eating. Some variety of whale, like. See?" He pointed as one of the creatures noisily ejected a long spray of water from the top of its head.

Yves had heard of whales, of course, and had known that there was some creature called a dolphin in the sea, but he had not been aware of any more detail than that. He watched more closely, noting the elegance and strength of the dolphins' movements, and the permanent, sardonic smile on their jaws full of tiny, sharp teeth.

Fid spoke again, tentatively. "Heard about your bunkmate. Guess he was a friend from before now?"

Yves nodded, not feeling equal yet to putting in words the friendship he'd had with Luc.

Fid didn't question him further, but after a few more minutes of watching the dolphins, he said suddenly, "Same thing happened to me, on my first voyage. Bunkmate took ill suddenly, and before the surgeon could find the right dose to bring him around, he was gone. Good man in a fight, and knew more about sailing that I've forgotten, even now."

Yves found his voice and said quietly, "I owe a great deal to Luc. He did for me when I could not do for myself, and . . . "

He paused. Taking a deep breath, he said, "I do not want to seem selfish, but his passing leaves me with debts of honor that I do not know how to repay."

Fid let the ocean and dolphins speak for a while before he finally replied, "I still think about Jean from time to time, wonder about his papa and brother—Jean always had stories about them—and hope that they're all right with him gone."

He turned to face Yves directly now. "But what I don't do, both for the sake of Jean's memory, and to avoid the sadness of it all myself, is to take on the burden of living Jean's life for him. My own life is a full enough bag of rocks, without dragging his along behind me as well. He wouldn't have wanted that of me, and there is no way that I could live up to it, even if he had."

He turned back to regard the setting Sun. "You're a good lad, Yves. You remind me a lot of a boy I used to see in the glass when I was shaving. I see you carrying around that load of your friend's death, and I wish I knew some way to slip it off your shoulders, so that you can stand up straight again."

He spat into the ocean as it slid past. "People come into our lives, and they leave our lives, but just because they're gone doesn't mean that they don't still matter. I'm not saying that at all. The fact that you knew your friend means that your life was changed for having known him. You can choose to make his death the thing that changes you, or you can choose to make it his life that changes you."

Yves didn't say anything, but he could almost feel a weight leave him as he thought about what Fid had said. There was great truth in it—Luc had been too full of life for his death to be the part of their friendship that Yves remembered above all else.

He nodded slowly and faced Fid. "Let me tell you about my friend Luc," he said.

Fid's face split into a big, jagged smile and he said, "Let's go down below, and I'll see if I can get the cook to serve us out a little extra grog to toast Luc's memory with."

Despite himself, Yves smiled back, and motioned for the sailor to lead the way.

Chapter 7

Every passing day brought the fleet further west, and as they appeared to be on a heading south of due west, there was speculation that they might be headed for the pestilence-ridden islands of the Indies. However, there was no official word as to their precise destination, and so the rumors remained nothing more than that.

The next sail the fleet spotted turned out to be a small English merchant, and she struck her colors after a short pursuit by one of the frigates. In what Yves thought had to be an even greater ignominy than being towed, the captured ship was deemed to be unworthy of crewing, even for its cargo, and after the men on board had been brought on board as captives, the warships were instructed to use her for cannon practice.

The soldiers on board the *Baron d'Arras* gathered along the rail to watch the big warships make sport of the hapless merchant, and they laughed and made bets on how many barrages she would withstand, how long she would take to break up, and whether any stowaway rats might escape.

"So long as they don't teach our rats to speak English, I will be glad enough," one wag declared.

Yves shuddered in memory and replied, "I care not what tongue our rats speak, only that they stay off my face as I sleep."

"Perhaps they already speak English, and we need to

learn enough of that language to instruct them on the etiquette of traveling over our hammocks when they are already occupied."

The soldiers roared in laughter, and then were distracted as the flagship lined up and fired a broadside at the English merchant ship. Several well-aimed balls struck along the waterline, and the little ship soon listed heavily as it began to wallow.

The next warship in the line had its turn, and when the smoke from the barrage had cleared, only the topmast of the merchant was still above water, and even that swiftly sank from view.

The bets were settled, with some good-natured ribbing in all directions, and as their ship sailed, still under tow, past the surprisingly small collection of flotsam that rode the waves marking the final resting place of the sunken hulk, they were gratified—or perhaps disappointed—to see no rats striving for a more reliable passage to *terra firma*.

Yves couldn't help but feel a tiny glimmer of sympathy for the putative rats on the English ship, destroyed by a catastrophe beyond their understanding or control. So it was, he supposed, with men at a time of war, whether they sank or swam.

A squall approached from the south, and Yves watched the bands of rainfall pouring out of it, looking like curtains draped beneath some sash floating through the evening sky. Not wanting to get soaked to the skin again, and having no duties pressed upon him this watch, he returned to the dank belowdecks where at least it was dry.

Under the hammock he had once shared with Luc, a small bundle containing his friend's clothing was all that remained of the man. Yves found himself wondering yet again at the future, and whether or not he might be granted the ability to fulfill Luc's final request—or even what good it might do if he did. Perhaps, at the very least, he could persuade one of their company who could write to take down a letter to be sent back to the girl.

He sighed as he heard the drumbeat of the rain start on the deck above his head, and climbed into his hammock. The familiar rocking of the ship as it continued through the water around, combined with the susurration produced by the water above, served to make it easier than usual to fall asleep.

In the morning, one of the warships ahead signaled that it had lost a man in the water; being at the end of the convoy, it fell to men of the *Baron d'Arras* to see whether the lost man could be recovered from the water, whether alive or dead.

It was a grim but effective diversion from the boredom that had overcome the men of the company, now that the crew of the privateer had settled into their duties, and their routine did not demand a great deal of the soldiers. They gathered at the rail to watch the sea slide past, alert for any hint of a man afloat, but saw nothing.

After many long minutes, the soldiers began to drift away from the rail and back belowdecks, where they could throw dice or play cards out of sight of their officers. For their part, Yves had noted that the officers likewise kept their games of chance out of view of the enlisted men, so as to avoid setting a bad example for the moral conduct of the company.

Yves did not particularly care for any of these games, and certainly had no extra coin to risk at them. However, there was little enough else to divert his attention from a perpetually grumbling gut, or the sheer ennui of shipboard life, so he at least observed the games of others around him.

As he watched a spirited game of dice on the lower deck, his mind wandered to the fate of the man who had fallen overboard. His death had been swift at least, as it was rare that even those who made their lives at sea knew how to swim even a few strokes. The terror of going over the side made this little world, bound by a few dozen feet in any direction, all the more precious to them.

How curious, he thought, that men should think to create a small area of dry land to carry themselves about the world, bringing with them everything that they might need for their comfort and survival. Comfort, though, he thought wryly, was a relative thing.

Certainly, though, no bird would be caught carrying about a nest under it, nor would a fish go for a stroll with a cup of water in tow. Only human beings were so hungry to see past the horizon that they were moved to perform such feats.

And yet, once inured to the miracle that they were standing on a dry space thousands of leagues distant from any land, with every expectation that they stood a good chance of seeing land again, they grew so bored by the condition that they had to invent ways to entertain themselves in the midst of this wonder.

He smiled to himself as he stood to depart the game, and returned above decks to watch the sea pass by and examine distant banks of clouds to see whether he could predict which might bear rain their way.

As he arrived on deck, he heard members of the crew laughing and shouting to one another, and saw the strangest sight he had yet beheld in all the days of his voyage. Scattered across the deck were small fish, flopping and gasping, and as he watched, he saw more flung up onto the deck, seemingly erupting from the sea of their own volition.

The crewmembers were gathering the fish from where they landed, and putting them into whatever containers could be pressed into service. One fish landed at Yves' feet, and he picked up and examined the creature, holding it behind the gills as his father had taught him to do, so that he could avoid being stabbed by any spines that the fish might have, no matter how much it struggled in his hand.

Elongated fins jutted out behind the gills, and the body of the fish was a bit longer than his hand. Its eyes were strangely oversized and stared at him accusingly as he held it. Fid passed by, bending and scooping the fish into a leather bucket, and called to Yves, "Have you tasted flying fish before?"

"Tasted them? I have never so much as heard a hint that such a wonder might exist! Do they truly fly?"

"Well, not so much flying as gliding, and they are wonderfully tasty fried in a little butter." He looked downcast for a moment, then brightened up as another fish flopped down onto the deck in front of him. "Cook won't spare any butter for the likes of us, of course, but they're still good just fried in themselves. So long as we clean the fish for him, and grant him a share in them for himself, he'll consent to do that much for us."

"Well, then I should only be too glad to help you gather them." He held out the fish he had picked up, and Fid rewarded him with a crooked smile as the leathern bucket jumped at the new addition.

Fid motioned over to the railing and said, "Come, let us see whether we can witness them launching out of the water."

Yves followed the sailor to the side of the ship, and was surprised to see that their escort of porpoises was back. Fid pointed and laughed, saying, "There, now we see why they fly. Those beasts pursue them, and the fish think to escape to the safety of our decks." He laughed, a mirthless sound. "Their lot would be better if they stayed in the water, of course, but fish are not usually known for their reasoning abilities."

He lifted the bucket up, gauging its weight. "Just a couple more and we'll have enough for a meal, I would think. You've a treat ahead of you!"

Yves laughed and scooped up a fish that had come to rest against the side of the belowdecks hatch. To think, he mused, that he might have missed out on this fun in favor of a game of dice. Life was interesting enough without having to invent ways to pass its few hours.

Chapter 8

Yves found hisdetermination to find fascination in the miracle of every moment severely strained over the course of the next several weeks of sailing. The routine seemed designed to make the miraculous feel like toil.

Wake with the bell, break his fast with meals that varied only in the degree of their awfulness, find someplace to be out of the way of the privateer's crew as they went about their duties, perhaps watch a squall approach to rock and wash down the ship, maybe hear of a sail on the horizon, or spot porpoises alongside the ship.

The fleet did catch another small British ship—a privateer without even guns mounted, more of a yacht than a serious prize—and there did come the day when the company's captain was summoned to the flagship to receive the confirmation of what all aboard had long assumed.

The company captain, when he returned, summoned his troops to stand in good order on the deck of the privateer as he read the unsealed order aloud. It started with some routine matters concerning pay, order of disembarkation, and the usual ominous threats regarding discipline amongst the ranks, laying out the punishments authorized for various forms of misconduct.

Then, however, he got to the meat of the orders, which confirmed much of what most members of the company already expected. The only surprise—and it was only a small one—was that they were sailing to North America and not the Indies, though where exactly they would land was still not disclosed. There, they would be officially serving as allies to the Americans' rebellious forces. Some of the details of the orders set the soldiers to buzzing amongst themselves.

After the company captain dismissed the troops, Yves heard one grizzled *bas-officier* muttering to another, "We are to subsume the white ribbons on our hats' cockades to additional ribbon of black, symbolizing that we are subordinate in every way to their command, and to respect their officer's orders as if they were our own?"

The second man nodded, adding, "They have even made it clear that in cases where ranks are equal, the man with the earlier date of birth will be the superior, without regard to whether he be French or American—and should we be equal in that matter as well, the American will be the senior."

He shook his head and spat over the railing of the ship. "Hired mercenaries then, we are to be, and not a proper fighting force under the commands of our King alone." A grin split his face. "And all those pretty words about paying for our supplies, and leaving their women alone? How long do you suppose those will last, once the cannon roar?"

His companion gave a snort. "Well, I know that no woman need fear some of these boys, but there are few women anywhere who are safe when we take the field, eh?" He slapped the second man's back, and the two of them shared a rolling guffaw. They chopped off as they noticed Yves standing nearby, and then the one whispered something to the other, gesturing at the younger soldier, and they started laughing all over again.

Yves turned away, wondering why the company's *bas-officiers* seemed hardly any more moral than the sailors on the privateer's crew. Perhaps they did not swear with quite as much vigor or blasphemy, and they may have been somewhat more clean about their persons, but could the company do no better than these men? Could not Luc have made a good and decent leader of men, or would the position of influence over their fates have turned him into a leering lout as well?

He sighed and went back below to see how the unceasing dice games were progressing, and to perhaps make some more time for sleep if the games were quiet enough. As he went down the hatch into the gun deck, he encountered Fid making his way up.

The sailor looked Yves over and asked, "What brings you to look as though you've been accused of killing a man . . . or might like to earn the accusation soon?"

Yves waved his hand dismissively. "I am but wishing that men's natures were better than they are. It is a hopeless wish, I know." He smiled without joy and shook his head.

Fid grinned at him and said, "If I didn't know better, I'd think you'd been brought up by a school of nuns. Myself, I let other men's natures be their own concern, and worry about my own nature. There's full enough to occupy my attention there, let me tell you."

When Yves did not return his grin, Fid said, "Of course, that's what works for me, and part of this philosophy of mine is also knowing that it don't work for all those around me. Some get a lot of pleasure out of judging the actions of others around them." He shrugged. "I have always held with the belief that judgment is not ours to pass, but the priests and inquisitors have felt otherwise, of course."

Yves favored the man with a sour frown. "I do believe that you just compared me to the Inquisition, and if that is not a form of judgment, I do not know what might be."

Fid did not return his frown, but instead became merrier still in his expression. "Why, so it is, and you have caught me on my own hook! I shall keep my own counsel then, and leave you to yours, whatever it might be."

Yves couldn't help but return the other man's smile, and he replied, "And you have indeed caught me on my own hook as well, for how am I to be so upstanding as to presume to judge my fellows, when the very act of such judgment renders me as immoral in my own way as they are in theirs."

A twinkle shone in Fid's eye as he said, "Careful, boy, or the priests will want a word with you for questioning the basis of their practice of the confession."

"Ah, well there's little danger of the return of the Inquisition, now is there? At least, not with the likes of you around to remind us of the proper role of morality." Yves smiled again and shook his head ruefully.

He would never have thought to be engaged in a conversation about morality and philosophy with a common sailor. Judging men by their station in life was a mistake that he would need to avoid in the future, he mused to himself. Somehow, he suspected that he might not remember this lesson as well as he ought to. He sighed and continued on his way belowdecks.

There, he encountered four soldiers struggling to carry a crate to the hatch. Looking at the markings on the side, Yves could make out that it held weapons, both muskets and swords. He frowned, asking curiously, "Why are you shifting these about?"

The man nearest him gasped out, "Orders," and took another step toward the crate, the other men struggling to keep pace with him.

"Shall I gather some more men, to make easier work of this task?" Yves was surprised to find himself feeling the initiative to make a sensible improvement, but then it only made sense for idlers to be put to work, when there was work to be done.

The man who'd spoken grunted, "Yeah, let's put this down for a minute, boys, while this fellow fetches some more hands to make lighter work of this."

Yves nodded in a friendly fashion and swarmed back up onto deck, where knots of soldiers still gathered, discussing the orders of the day. He approached the nearest group and said, "You men, there's a crate to be brought onto deck. Would you come with me to help your fellows do it more quickly?"

The soldiers turned to him, skepticism etched on nearly all of their faces. One asked incredulously, "What, are you a *bas-officier* now?"

Yves flushed red and said, "No, I am but a common soldier who has seen a need and is trying to answer it. If you are not interested, I will find some who are."

Another in the group said, "No, no, *monsieur Ledisciple*, do not take us that way. We will be glad to help." He glanced at the first man who'd spoken, who now scowled. "Well, perhaps not glad, but we'll still do it, if it needs to be done."

Most of the group followed Yves to the open hatch and followed him down to where the original four men still stood at the corners of the crate. As many as could get a firm grip on it lined up around, and lifted it easily, pushing it overhead to the edge of the hatch, where, with a final heave, it tipped and landed with a bang onto the deck.

"Thank you," said the man with whom Yves had originally spoken. "I'll go and let the lieutenant know that the work is done, and that the company will have arms, should the need arise in the days to come." Yves nodded to him as the men who'd assisted wandered off to their own interests on the ship, lest someone find some more work for them to do.

Only the soldier who had rallied the group on deck to follow Yves' suggestion remained behind. Offering Yves his hand, he said, "*Monsieur Ledisciple*, I do not believe that we have properly introduced ourselves to one another before. I am Gerard Beauchene *dit Saugues*, and I served with your friend Luc in the West Indies. We did not see eye to eye on many things, Luc and I, but I grieved his death along with you, and appreciate your care for him in his final agonies."

Yves took the other man's hand, somberly replying, "It was my duty and my honor to attend him at the last, and I only wish that I could have preserved him so that you could have been granted the time to resolve your differences with him. He was a worthy friend, and a good man. Please, call me Yves."

Gerard smiled gently. "Perhaps too good. In any event, you seem to have learned well from his example how to encourage men to do your will."

Yves shook his head dismissively. "I did no more than what anyone would have done, seeing those fellows straining at that crate."

Gerard shrugged. "And yet you did it, and the task is

complete under your suggestion. If you are not careful, you will find yourself earning a promotion to *bas-officier*, once the bullets begin to fly and their ranks are thinned."

Yves snorted and said, "I do not think that I have the low morals or poor manners to fulfill such a role, in the unlikely event it should be offered to me."

Gerard laughed, saying only, "Time will tell, Yves. Time will tell."

Chapter 9

Yves first heard the beating of the drums from the warship ahead of him from belowdecks. A rush of activity over his head made it very clear that it was something different from prior alarms and certainly not routine activity.

Crewmembers swarmed into the belowdecks and started cutting down the hammocks, without regard for whether they were occupied or not. One soldier protested, shouting from the floor where he'd been unceremoniously dumped, "What is the purpose of this fresh abuse?"

The sailor paused long enough to shout in answer, "We are to clear this gun deck for action at once. Six sail have been spotted, and they are English ships of war. We are headed for battle!"

Another sailor added, "The bunch of you ought to go on deck and arm yourselves, to see if you can be of some use there. You've guns and swords; issue them out and pray they're not needed."

The soldiers of the company jumped into motion quickly at this news, and within a few minutes, they were queued up at the weapon crates, with their captain handing out a gun and a sword to each man.

His *bas-officiers* were forming up their squads and directing them to places on the deck where the crew had indicated that they would have the best vantage for firing at the enemy, while hindering the sailors as little as possible as they fought the ship.

Yves could see that the fleet had re-formed itself from a stretched-out convoy into a tightly-ordered arrangement, with the lightly-armed troop ships in the lee of the warships, which fairly bristled with cannon, all trained on the English as they approached.

He noticed, with wonder, that the flagship and other warships flew the English pennant, and was struck by the seeming poor conduct that this represented. Should they attempt to beguile the enemy into approaching within range of their guns by the use of such a dishonest tactic? Was all naval warfare so dishonorable and deceitful?

A pair of the warships from the fleet was pursuing a single ship that had broken away from the enemy formation. Yves jumped at the crack of the cannon, followed by a rolling boom, like that of thunder, as one of the French ships fired at the English straggler. Evidently, the admiral considered the ruse penetrated then, transparent though it had been, and the faux English pennants came down, replaced immediately with the white French flags.

The battle was begun in earnest now, and Yves was amazed at how much like the choreography of a dance in a ballroom it seemed, with ships wheeling about and flashing sails up and down as they sought advantage of position over one another. The mood on the privateer was tense but confident.

He heard the crewmen speaking to each other, pointing out the movements of the various ships arrayed across the ocean before them, commenting on how strong their fleet's numbers were in comparison with the enemy's, and how disordered the English fleet's movements seemed to be in contrast to the sharply-executed maneuvers of the French fleet.

In their disorder, though, the English stayed upwind of the French fleet, which, Yves gathered from the crewmen's excited comments, gave them an advantage in maneuvering . . . though it appeared to Yves' untrained eye to that they were failing to press this advantage.

The English came at the fleet in a straight line, the maws of their cannon aimed at the big warships of the French naval forces. A broadside spit fire in their direction, and in spite of himself, Yves ducked down as far as he could, until he sheepishly noticed that the privateer's crewmen around him remained upright, craning for a better view.

The sound came then, as if an entire forest had been felled just past the windows of a cottage, with a coordinated set of closely-spaced cracks, followed by the long, low boom that echoed weirdly among the ships of the fleet.

The ships responded to signals from the great flagship, and wheeled about to flank the English, who also came about to exchange another volley with their enemies. Again, the smoke of cannon fire rose, this time originating from the French. The English answered, and the rippling crack and boom of the engagement rolled over the *Barron d'Arras* and the men on her decks, sailor and soldier alike.

When the smoke had cleared enough to make an assessment, no appreciable damage could be seen with the naked eye, though the ship's captain looked through his glass and called out to the men that the fire had carried away the bowsprit of one of the English ships. A cheer went up among the crew at this word, but the mood remained tense.

The English again wheeled about, but the commander of the

French fleet declined to press his pursuit into the swiftly gathering gloom of the evening, and the English sailed away at great speed, all sails raised. Yves could hear angry muttering among the men of the ship's crew, but he could hear, too, a note of relief in their voices.

As for the soldiers, they were glad enough to return their weapons to their cases, and to have escaped the need to try their hands at close combat onboard that most unnatural of battlefields, the deck of a ship at sea.

Fid approached, his mouth in a deep frown. Seeing Yves, he said without preamble, "I hope that *monsieur* de Ternay has disengaged from those English dogs for some reason better than being shy of battle, particularly when hindered by a great convoy made up of the likes of us."

Yves' brow beetled, and he answered, "Were we a great hindrance? It looked to my innocent eye as though we, and the rest of the fleet, maneuvered well, and kept our positions well and followed orders with alacrity."

Fid made a diffident motion with his hands and said, "We did well enough, it is true. But a fleet of warships such as these, without the concerns of wallowing cargo tubs, would have pursued those English ships to the edge of the ocean, until every one of them either struck its colors, or sat on the bottom."

He scowled and added under his breath, "The prize money would have been welcome as well, what little of it might have made it to my pockets."

Yves frowned. "I have heard the crewmen speak of prize money before, as though it were a natural part of your pay, but it has never been clearly explained to me."

Fid grinned and said, "Ah, then you will better appreciate why we hope so much for the capture of enemy ships. Whenever the fleet takes a worthwhile enemy ship, we send it back to France to the prize court, where, once they have ascertained that the prize was taken legally, they sell it into service, or to the highest bidder, should it not be fit for naval duty. The proceeds of that sale are then divided among the crews responsible for the capture, according to our rank and position."

Yves smiled in understanding. "Ah, then you stand to gain personally from any action that takes place in the course of our voyage."

"Yes, though with a small prize like that yacht that we took some weeks back, it amounts to a pittance. A fleet such as we lost today, though, would have meant some real money, even divided as many ways as it would be." He sighed. "Ah, well such prizes are invariably bought with blood, and we have little enough of that to go around."

Motioning to the landsmen returning belowdecks to restore their hammocks and sort out their possessions from where they had been hastily pushed aside, he said, "Too, what we mean to deliver to the American shores is likely worth more to the commanders than nearly any prize we might encounter."

Yves gave him a sour smile, not liking being so obviously considered as little more than living cargo. He nodded, though, and said, "I hope that you are all richly rewarded for your sacrifice, my friend."

Fid bowed his head in a mocking salute, and went on to his duties. Yves followed the other soldiers belowdecks, where he found several crewmen efficiently knotting the hammocks back into place, replacing the sliced away lines as needed. His small rucksack of clothing was readily at hand in the heap of belongings that had been retrieved from whatever corner they had occupied during the excitement.

Within a matter of minutes after the ship had canted over to follow the rest of the fleet into the darkness to the East, Yves was securely in his hammock, drifting off to a peaceful and uneventful sleep.

Chapter 10

Yves stepped onto the sand and was surprised to find himself feeling unsteady on his feet, as the ground beneath them did not move with the waves, but instead stayed firm. He tossed his head to shake off the feeling, and felt his teeth rattle against each other, so loose were they in his jaw from the scurvy that seemed to afflict every other man who had sailed.

Picking his way more carefully along the beach, he followed the *bas-officiers*, who were exhorting everyone to move faster, ever faster, lest some officer of the company think that they were slacking in their duties to keep the men miserable.

The last few weeks of the voyage had provided misery enough, in Yves' opinion, and there was little need for the *bas-officiers* to add to it in any regard. The water had spoiled, leaving only the daily tot of rum drinkable. What food remained had, as Luc had predicted, only gotten more flavorless, save for the creeping flavor of rancidness that had overcome everything they ate or drank.

More English patrols had disrupted the fleet's progress, and though many of these patrols had come to grief at the guns of the French warships, the possibility of attack at any moment had transformed boredom into a long-running and endless exercise in tension, as though holding oneself stiff against a blow that might or might not land at any moment.

When the other ships of the fleet had nearly vanished into thick fog, in addition to the real possibility that the enemy might approach undetected—a fear that had been realized in the cover of darkness before they encountered the fog—there was also the danger of colliding with another ship of the fleet, or, as they approached the North American continent, even land.

Worse, they could become separated from the fleet and bumble about the English-infested waters, at constant risk of encountering a superior force. One of the other troop carriers was lost in the fog and never seen again, taking with it hudreds of soldiers, their fates unknown.

Between these hazards, the crewmen on the privateer were now as tense as any of the soldiers of the company, and that, combined with the outbreak in earnest of scurvy, meant that tempers were also at a breaking point. An argument over dice became an outright brawl, and even the strict enforcement of the previously lax ban on games of chance had failed to patch up the resentments that simmered among the men crammed into narrow decks of the privateer.

Yves had found himself wondering how he had ever come to consider the floating bit of dry space in the midst of the ocean any form of miracle at all. It seemed, instead, to have been devised with the deliberate goal of inflicting the greatest possible misery on the most possible men at the least possible cost to King and country.

But—he reminded himself as he marched up the sand with his company—that was all in his past, and he was now in a country full of grateful, well-provisioned, and cheerful people. As the ships had passed the first point of land, there had been cheering both aboard ship and from the shore, and any sort of conceivable wonder seemed possible.

The company fell into step together once they got off the sand, the crunch of their shoes in unison as they swung along. Yves examined the fair and battered place to which the miserable voyage had brought them.

Even after years of warfare, Yves could see that the streets of the little town were lined with neat, well-constructed houses, and—wonder of wonders—most of the inhabitants who gathered at their stoops to wave and wish the newcomers welcome seemed to be young women. What men were in evidence were old and past military service, or too young themselves to have yet answered the martial call of their newborn nation's need.

Some of the houses had been fired or simply knocked to pieces, and Yves presumed that had happened over the course of the English occupation of the island, recently ended by the arrival of a previous French expedition. Too, there were almost no trees standing in the town, though there were many stumps to be seen, evidence of a careless ravaging of the countryside by its occupiers.

The lieutenant leading the men of the company directed them to what appeared to be a campsite abandoned by the English when they had departed the prior autumn, in the wake of a great battle against the French and American forces. Yves was curious about the details of that battle . . . and whether the English had any designs upon returning to re-take their former place.

What gear the soldiers did not carry themselves was brought along by companies of boys and a handful of slaves offered for service to the company by residents of the town. Yves had only seen a few moors back home, and he tried not to be too familiar in his gaze as he looked at them, filled with curiosity.

Most of them were strongly built, and clearly shaped by the heavy labor in which they were routinely employed. For the most part, they said nothing at all to the French soldiers, and when they did speak, Yves guessed it was in English, though he could not understand it. Of course, he reflected, he spoke the language but a little, with a few phrases memorized from lessons given by the older men of the company, and crewmen from the *Baron d'Arras*, who assured him that their broad experience of the American colonies encompassed much of its language.

He was certain that asking for a latrine or rum would be useful; commenting on the weather somewhat less so. When Fid had laughingly made him repeat after him the words that he promised would get a kiss out of any American girl, Yves had thought they were unlikely to be of any use to him on his arrival.

Now, he wasn't so sure, though he still entertained doubts as to whether Fid could be entirely trusted about the certainty of success. He had heard similar claims about girls back home, using phrases in the language he had been born to, and had never enjoyed any victories under those more promising circumstances.

Still, the people who had turned out to welcome the French back to this little town had been enthusiastic, and with the proportion who were of the gentler sex, he wondered whether he might have an opportunity in the weeks to come to at least try the unfamiliar words.

As Yves worked with a group of men to raise one tent after another, taking advantage where possible of the remnants of hearths and the dug-in floor areas, a *bas-officier* approached the group and pointed at him, apparently at random.

"You. You're with me, to fetch rations for the mess." Yves

shrugged at the other men working on pulling the oilcloth over the poles they'd just notched and set into place, and let go of his section of the heavy fabric.

He followed the *bas-officier*, who hurried along the road back into town. As he strode along, he said over his shoulder, "I am Sergeant Chartiere, but so long as we are not in the company of others, you may call me Henri. You are . . . ?"

"Yves de Bourganes *dit Ledisciple*, sir, and most just call me by my *nom de guerre*."

"Don't call me sir," Henri snapped, adding with a sardonic smile, "I work for a living." He continued to walk briskly down the road, and Yves struggled to match his stride.

When he was in step with the sergeant, he found himself puffing to keep up, but he maintained the pace for several minutes. Henri turned as he walked and regarded Yves curiously.

"Did you do nothing aboard the ship for the purpose of maintaining your wind?"

"No, s—, I mean, Henri, nothing beyond the few tasks assigned to me by my superiors." He left unstated that he was grateful that the other man had not been among the superiors assigning him tasks.

"That's a shame, and your superiors were derelict in their duties by failing to ensure that you would step off that ship ready at once to face the English, had they challenged us upon our arrival to these shores."

Yves frowned, unhappy with what the man was pointing out. "Henri, half of our men are yet weak from the scurvy, and had we not reached these shores at the moment when we did, I assure you that no English bullets would have been needed to put most of them into their graves."

Henri stopped abruptly, his head cocked to one side as he regarded Yves. He nodded briskly and said, "You are right, of course, but one doesn't normally tell even a lowly sergeant that he is so fundamentally wrong. You must learn diplomacy, *monsieur Ledescaple.*" His mouth twitched as though he were enjoying a private joke at Yves' expense.

"It's *Ledisciple,* sir," Yves corrected the other man, who looked at him reprovingly.

"Clearly, you also need to learn to listen, *monsieur Ledisciple.*" He laughed, though, and added, "You will learn much before we leave this country. It is a marvelous place for teaching lessons, both those intended and some along the way."

He stopped suddenly, and Yves heard what the other man had fallen silent to listen to. It was a woman's voice, strident and angry, and it sounded as though she was on the edge of committing some awful violence, from her tone. It appeared to be emanating from a nearby baker's shop, and Yves had to hurry again to keep up with Henri as he strode in the direction of the unpleasant sounds.

The two of them rounded the corner just in time to see a young boy hurled into the street, followed by several chunks of bread, thrown with such force that they bounced off his head and back, and clear to the other side of the street. The boy scrambled to his feet, retrieved the nearer chunk of bread, and was gone, ducking into the space between the baker's shop and the next building on the street.

Henri, with Yves trailing behind him, walked into the baker's shop, doffing his hat and bowing respectfully before the woman who stood at the door, her nostrils still flaring, and her hair wildly escaping from under her cap. "*Madame,*" he said, his hand sweeping toward the floor in an elegant salute, "*Je m'appelle Sergeant Chartiere; parlez-vous français?*"

The phrase with which she responded in English was not one of those which Yves had memorized, but from her scowl, he was relatively sure that it was meant to be rude.

That she not only refused to acknowledge or return Henri's bow reinforced this impression. She spat past his proffered hand, and turned away, bustling into the back room of the baker's shop.

Henri straightened, turned to Yves and, with a cocked eyebrow, said, "I will take it that she does not speak French then, and furthermore that she does not have an interest in selling us any bread."

He sighed and asked, "Do you suppose that she could throw me into the street as well as she did that urchin?" Yves shrugged, and the other man grinned. "Well, let us find out then."

He went around the counter and began gathering up loaves of bread into one arm, tucking them like firewood into the crook of his elbow. As he did so, the woman reappeared from the back room and shrieked at him. This time, Yves was pretty sure that he caught one of the words she spat out, and recognized it from the phrase that Fid had taught him. Definitely not a good idea to try that phrase, without knowing exactly what he was saying.

Henri made his escape around the far end of the counter, and waved Yves out the door ahead of him, dodging stale bread rolls that the woman was now hurling at him. "Go, go," he urged Yves, laughing and clutching at the bread he'd stolen.

Together, they ran back away from town, slowing only when the woman gave up her pursuit, slowed by unshod feet. The stream of invective she shouted after the two hardly needed translation, and Yves wasn't sure that it would be safe to ever again pass by her door without an armed force to accompany him.

Chapter II

When Yves and Henri topped a small rise opening the view to the camp, they were still chortling to each other over the woman at the baker's shop. At a glance, though, they could see that the camp was not as they had left it. Everything was in a state of utter chaos, with men scurrying in every direction, squads hurriedly throwing up earthworks, and teams hauling what guns had been unloaded from the ships into defensive positions.

Sergeant Chartiere asked a passing lieutenant, "Sir, what is the cause of this commotion, and where do you need myself and this soldier to go, to be of the most use?"

The officer paused just long enough to blurt, "Twenty-one sail of warships spotted approaching the channel, and it is anticipated that they will try our defenses at once!" He turned immediately and continued on his way, tossing over his shoulder, "Go at once to your stations; look for your messmates."

Chartiere said under his breath to Yves, "I think I can spare the moment to bring this bread to the kitchens, as the men will need to eat even more in the midst of all this action. I only wish we could have brought more. You, go ahead to your mess, and may the saints preserve you, come what may."

Yves nodded curtly, replying, "And you as well, Sergeant Chartiere," before he left at a run to find Gerard and the other men of his mess.

They were engaged in shoveling dirt and rocks into a rough breastwork, and Yves found a shovel in the bottom of the crate in which they'd been shipped. He fell into place beside Gerard, and took up the well-practiced routine of piling soil quickly and efficiently to provide a shield against incoming musket shot.

He knew from experience in training that they would be unlikely to stop a cannon ball with such a makeshift earthwork, but it was possible that the English would hold off their attack long enough to raise more durable fortifications.

Two more companies, *chausseurs* and *grenadiers*, arrived on the neck of land where Yves' company was so intensely laboring. The *grenadiers* were, to a man, enormous specimens, though their numbers were strangely few. Yves had heard that this was owing to the greater propensity for these large men to fall ill with scurvy.

Regardless of their reduced numbers, they were eagerly welcomed into the crews shifting gun emplacements about. The English had left behind some bedraggled earthworks, and some in surprisingly good condition; all were a welcome starting point in defending against their return.

Yves was already feeling the fatigue of a sudden bout of exercise after a long period of forced inactivity when he'd arrived back at camp, and this heavy labor was quickly exhausting him to the point of collapse.

He was clearly not the only man in the company who was suffering, and when one man finally did pass out with a dull thud onto the sand, a *bas-officier* Yves did not recognized walked over to the group of men and motioned with his thumb to the kitchens.

"Go, take a meal, and grab some rest. You'll be back on

the line in one hour. Meanwhile, send those fellows over." He motioned to one of the newly-arrived squads of *chausseurs*. With a start, one of the men in that group noticed that the *bas-officier* was summoning them, and called out to his fellows.

The men lined up and marched over in good order, while Yves' group stumbled away toward the kitchens. Yves couldn't help but notice that the newcomers' uniforms were neatly turned out, despite having endured the same hardships for which their company commander had excused their appearance.

As he followed his company-mates over to the kitchen tents, Yves looked over his shoulder to see the newly-arrived *chausseurs* lining up crisply to recover the shovels dropped all over the entrenchment, and then stepping forward nearly in unison to continue the work.

Gerard was watching, too, and snorted derisively, "Martinets. Their formation is pretty, but we'll see how much real work they get done."

Yves smiled at his friend, saying, "They look pretty effective to me."

"I'll bet you a Spanish dollar that they are in a confusion by the time we return, and further that they will have completed no more of the wall than we have prior to getting this period of rest."

Yves shook his head ruefully. "I wish that I had a Spanish dollar to put to chance with you, my friend, for I am confident that I would have two by the setting of the sun."

Gerard laughed. "Ah, well neither have I, so you would in truth have been no further ahead had you won the bet." He ducked under the mouth of the kitchen tent and sniffed suspiciously. "I wonder what horrors the cooks have awaiting us today?"

One of the cooks looked up at him with a scowl. "I heard that, you ungrateful lout. Some time, you ought to try to feed so many men with so few supplies."

Gerard shrugged. "I had heard that the local people were eager to trade with us for the supplies we need."

The cook retorted, "Not that I have seen so far. What we have is what we brought, save that we now enjoy fresh water instead of spoiled. The townsfolk may be willing to supply us, but it has not yet come to pass."

Yves suppressed a snort, and Gerard favored him with a tight scowl. "Have you and that sergeant so soon managed to turn the townsfolk against us, then?"

Yves shook his head, a sardonic smile on his face. "No, the one I encountered was not opposed to the French in specific, but seemed to be at war with all humankind in general. In any event, though she was not disposed to trade with us, the sergeant managed to, erm, secure some of her bread for our plates."

The cook held up his hands, empty as though to demonstrate that he had no bread. "None came to my hands," he said. "Perhaps the *bas-officiers* claimed what you brought for themselves?"

"In truth, we did not bring back very much, so I should not be surprised that there is none for the likes of us." Yves frowned thoughtfully. "I only wish that I had picked up one of the rolls with which she bombarded us as we made our departure from her shop."

Gerard slapped Yves on the back, laughing aloud. "I knew that there was more to the story of your sudden return from town with that sergeant. I thought perhaps that you had gotten word of the English fleet's arrival, but I see now that it was a more local and immediate threat that sent you pelting back to town."

Yves smiled enigmatically and shook his head. Addressing the cook, he said, "Friend, what have you to offer us, before we must return to striving at the trenchworks?"

The cook held out a battered tin plate and scooped up a ladle full of gruel, pouring it with exaggerated delicacy onto the plate. "For your first course, we tonight offer a fillet of cod, boiled until it will challenge no weak tooth you may be guarding, and with the addition of oats and plenty of fresh, sweet water. Your second course, should you be so lucky, will comprise more of the same. I sorrow to report that we do not have a dessert available this evening, but perhaps some sea-grass will settle your stomach." His mocking speech finished, the man held the plate out to Yves with a flourish.

Yves grimaced and accepted the plate, sniffing it hesitantly. He shook his head slowly and pursed his mouth grimly. He said to the cook, "If the labor does not kill me, and the English somehow spare me, I am reassured to know that you will still finish me before the year is out."

The cook gave a theatrical bow and answered, "At your service as always, sir."

Gerard snorted and held out his hand for a plate. "Had I wanted humor, I would have visited those rule-and-order men who are engaged in finishing our work for us over there."

Yves looked over to the earthwork, where the well-ordered company of *chausseurs* was still busy at work, their movements visibly synchronized, and their progress, even just since Yves had followed the rest of his company to the kitchens, was already apparent and substantial. He wished that he had taken the bet, and that Gerard had been good for it.

As they found a place to stand out of the way and eat the meal, such as it was, Sergeant Chartiere appeared. He gave Yves a tight, secret smile and said, "I see that you, too, were robbed of the bread that we stole fairly for the benefit of the company. I do not doubt but that the cooks saved it for themselves, the wretches."

Gerard snorted again. "Yves, stealing? I would never have believed it, had I not heard it from the lips of a *bas-officier* myself."

The sergeant gave Gerard a guarded look. "In truth, the man did none of the stealing himself, but only served to distract the shopkeeper long enough that I might relieve her of some stale and undesirable old bread."

Gerard laughed. "You need not defend my friend as though he stood for a court-martial, sir; I just know that his character is one of excessive honesty and painfully good morals."

Yves blushed, and Chartiere tried to speak, but Gerard continued, "I cannot tell you how much good it does my heart to see him come under the influence of one who can educate him more honestly in the ways of the world. I should like to know your name, sir, and to shake your hand."

Chartiere bowed slightly and said, "I ask that you not call me 'sir,' as I own no commission nor any title. My name is Sergeant Chartiere, and I am heartened also to see that our friend Yves has friends upon whom he may rely to testify as to his upstanding and honorable character."

Gerard took the sergeant's hand, bowed over it formally, and both men burst into laughter. When he could speak again, Gerard said, "Did I lead you astray in recommending *Monsieur*

Le disciple?"

"No, indeed, you did not; he served his role admirably."

Yves stood looking from one man to the other. Finally, he said incredulously, "You two know each other already?"

Gerard grinned and answered, "Indeed, we were promoted into the ranks of the *bas-officiers* at the same time. Henri found the position to his liking, while I found it too constricting to my vices and predilections."

Henri laughed and said, "Your friend Gerard here was the first one of our company to be both promoted and demoted in the course of a single day. It was a day that epics should celebrate, if only we could confess to half of the antics he undertook before the lieutenant caught up with him and stripped his rank."

Gerard laughed in turn. "Alas, it is still too soon to make a full accounting of my sins that day, for the courts-martial could yet be convened for my benefit."

Yves was glad to have friends of such good cheer under the circumstances of the threat of imminent destruction at the hands of the English, but he was not convinced that they were good influences in matters of military discipline.

Chapter 12

What a difference a fortnight could make in the attitude of a fighting force, Yves marveled, looking over the encampment where he and his fellow soldiers had labored, both day and night, watch on and watch off, to dig in a secure position. Tidy rows of tents now stood secure behind solid entrenchments, and the colonel's banner snapped in the breeze that blew in from the ocean.

Where once they had supped on vermin-infested ship's supplies and what oddments that could be snatched up as they hurriedly passed through town, they now dined on rich stews of maize and even fresh meat no less than once a week.

Too, rum could be had in town, in addition to that which was supplied as part of their daily rations, and sweet fresh water was available in any desired quantity. Indeed, Yves could not remember ever having been so well provisioned, even before his father's death.

Better yet, the English fleet that had hovered outside of the bay for better than ten days finally raised anchor and sailed away. While it was likely that it would be a source of mischief to the American cause wherever else it was bound, everyone in the expedition had shared a sense of relief when the cluster of English sails were lost over the horizon.

Yves had written a long and cheerful letter to his mother,

with the assistance of a corporal who could write in a clear hand. The man had not had enough time to take down a letter to Luc's girl, but Yves resolved to have him write to her at the next such opportunity. He had entrusted the letter home to a brig that was dispatched to carry both official and personal correspondence back home to France. However, he had shared in the general dismay when the courier had run aground and sunk in plain view of everyone in the main body of the French encampment.

He'd heard that the pilot had been attempting to elude the English patrols that still lurked, and was in chancier waters than he ordinarily would have attempted. By grace and quick action, the crew was saved, but official dispatches, journals, and letters all were lost to the sea.

Yves was reassured that word of their safe arrival would make it to his mother's ears through official dispatches sent overland to ports safer for French activity, but he was nonetheless saddened that his own words would not reach his family.

Outside of that, however, his satisfaction with his conditions was nearly complete. The company drilled daily, of course, and there was always something that could be improved upon in their accommodations, but for the most part, his days were spent at relative ease.

The quiet did not suit everyone, however. Several officers from the company had already found offense between them over one thing or another—some was doubtless based on resentments developed over the course of their voyage—and had engaged in forbidden duels to settle their disputes. Both the surgeon and the commander were kept busy dealing with the aftermath of these fights.

For his part, Yves had watched a couple of duels, but he did not see the honor in standing up to let another man blast away at oneself. Moreover, if there were shots to be fired, they ought be aimed at the enemy, rather than at one's fellow soldiers. The commanders of the regiment agreed, and survivors of these duels were treated with quite harsh punishment.

As discipline had tightened up somewhat, the command came down from the generals that all provisions would be properly purchased with hard money. Thinking back to the shrieking woman at the baker's shop, Yves couldn't bring himself to feel guilty for Henri's opportunism, but he understood that a repeat performance of that type would not be tolerated.

Somehow, too, word of their exploits had gotten up the chain of command, and Yves and Henri found themselves unofficially confined to their encampment. Nothing formal was said, but when other men had a few hours' liberty to explore the environs of their fortification, the officers always found something pressing for the two of them to attend to.

It was, therefore, a surprise when he and Gerard were summoned to be part of a squad that was assigned to go and look at horses for the hussars. Yves had no particular expertise, but if they found suitable mounts for their use, he could lead a team of horses back to the encampment readily enough.

Gerard, it developed, had grown up around horses, and his uncle had even been the procurer for a troop of horse, so he thought that he had some idea of what to look for in a good warhorse. They were in the company of a *bas-officier* of the hussars, though, an enormous man who seemed little interested in Gerard's input, and spoke to the two soldiers only in brief commands.

The three of them set out, following directions given to them by an adjutant assigned to the American generals who had recently arrived in the encampment.

Clearly made nervous by the hussar's sheer physical presence, he said hesitantly, "Be sure to avoid the eastern shore, as we have heard that English patrols have sometimes landed there to take prisoners, and they are particularly interested in seizing French troops, if they can." The *bas-officier* snorted.

The adjutant cleared his throat and continued, "You know what your budget is, and how many men are to be provided for. This letter will provide assurance of payment in hard currency from the treasury of France, via the general, to any with whom you may strike a bargain." He handed the *bas-officier* a page bearing Rochambeau's personal seal. Even the big man's attitude became respectful as he accepted it with a bow.

"We shall use all diligence required to ensure that the men are supplied as they need, without needlessly expending the King's gold or the *Compte's* goodwill among these people." The hussar bowed again and turned abruptly, slipping the letter into his vest and striding out into the road, leaving Yves and Gerard to catch up with him.

Chapter 13

The road to the stables where they were to look at horses for the hussars passed by the baker's shop, and Yves cringed inwardly as they passed. The woman from whom Henri had stolen bread was not in evidence, but the young boy she had tossed out of her shop was sitting with his back to the wall of the building, occupying himself with a tree branch he had broken down until it was shaped roughly like a musket.

As the soldiers passed, the boy raised the branch to his shoulder and sighted down its length at them, making explosive sounds with his mouth as he picked the three of them off, one by one, with imaginary musket balls. Yves surmised that the baker woman passed along to the boy her obviously low opinion of the French troops.

Unwounded by the child's imagination, they went on their way to the stables, which consisted of a tidy horse barn adjoined by a field where a surprisingly large number of horses were grazing. Beside the door to the barn, an anxious-looking young man stood waiting for them, and the *bas-officier* bowed before him, the plumes in his hat swaying as he stood. The soldier introduced himself to the young man, speaking English in what sounded to Yves' untrained ear like a smooth and confident tone. He heard his name and Gerard's in the words that the soldier spoke, and the horse seller nodded to each of them in greeting.

Gerard, who had a bit more English than did Yves, leaned over and said, "He just introduced himself as Corporal Braun, and gave this fellow our names as well." Yves nodded in acknowledgment, eager to get the preliminaries out of the way. In the darkness of the barn, he could hear horses nickering, and a breeze carried the pungent smell of the animals to him. While his family had never been able to afford a horse, even while his father was alive, Yves had always felt drawn to them. When he'd joined the company, he had secretly hoped to be assigned to the hussars, but meeting just a few of those oversized troops had shattered those hopes and, in time, he had concluded that he was happy enough to be a *chausseur*.

Braun noticed that his attention was directed toward the barn and turned toward Yves and Gerard. With a brusque jerk of his head, he said, "Go in, if you like, and look." He turned back to the horse seller, and continued speaking with him in English. The seller made a quick comment and Braun added, "Never mind the blackbird. She's harmless."

Yves and Gerard grinned at each other and hurried in to visit with the horses within. In the first stall along the wide hall down the middle of the barn was a tired-looking old grey nag, her back swayed slightly with her years. She stood with her head over the gate to her stall, and her ears flicked forward at their approach. Her eyes were calm and patient-looking, and as he looked into them, Yves said, "We should have brought some sort of treats for the beasts, shouldn't we have?"

Gerard, reaching up and scratching gently behind the old mare's ears, answered, "Yes, but this old girl understands. Don't you, sweet thing?" He crooned at the old horse for a moment longer and then said, "What other animals are there? This nag's not going to be of any use to the hussars." Yves paused for a moment as he passed to add a scritch behind the horse's velvet-soft ears.

Pulling himself away from the contented animal, Yves continued into the darkness, where the next stall was occupied by a proud, strong-looking brown beast, whose shoulder was higher than his own. This horse was not waiting at the gate to be petted or treated, but instead was restlessly pacing about his stall, shoving his nose into a nearly-empty manger in the corner and returning to the front of the stall, where he looked at the two men with what appeared to be an expression of skepticism, tossing his head for a moment before returning to his hay.

Gerard looked at the animal and remarked, "Might be too flighty for our purposes, but certainly strong enough." He reached up with the intent of stroking the horse's nose, but jumped back as the animal bit at him, just missing his fingers. It settled for dipping its head to the gate of its stall and nibbling at a well-worn timber across the top. It appeared that the beast had been working at the wood for some time, and Yves could see significant damage to it. He laughed and said, "Definitely suitable for the hussars—man and beast would have to keep each other in line, though."

He moved down the line of stalls to the next one, where two coal-black horses stood side-by-side along the gate, barely visible in the darkness of the barn. As Yves approached, he had to suppress a gasp—these horses were simply enormous. Both of their shoulders were above his eye level, and their broad, strongly-built necks looked as though they were made to carry a wagon yoke. Gerard was already speaking quietly to the one closer to the corridor, and Yves frowned, trying to shake off the impression that the horse was actually listening to the man, and understanding him.

A noise from deeper within the building drew his attention and he called out, "Who is there?"

From the darkness of the stall behind them, a young woman whose skin was nearly black as the giant horses stepped forward. She spoke a few words in English, her tone of voice exhibiting a mixture of confusion and concern, and Gerard turned away from his examination of the horses to answer. Yves peered at her as Gerard spoke with her, though she was mostly invisible in the dimness of the barn.

They conversed for a few moments, and then Gerard said to Yves, "This is the slave that the horse seller had the corporal tell us about. I explained that we are here with the intent of buying some horses for our company, and she's offered to show us the ones that she guesses her master intends to offer to us."

Gerard chuckled and added, "We shall see whether his idea of suitable matches ours, of course. We need stronger, calmer horses than a mere coach-and-four will require, and for riding, they will have to be of strong back and good wind." He reached back to pat one of the huge horses, saying, "I wish we had had these fellows when we were hauling cannon with our own backs. They are made for that sort of labor, where our troops are not."

Yves laughed briefly and answered, "Doubtless, the captain was just as happy to save the coin for as long as he could. No matter that half the troops were mostly dead from the trip here." His tongue involuntarily ran over his teeth yet again, testing them to see if they had recovered from their scurvy-caused looseness.

The slave gestured to them and led them out of the far end of the barn and through a gate into the field that surrounded the building on three sides.

In the light, Yves noticed for the first time that her clothing consisted of little more than rags, and he felt his face flush hot as he realized that she was in a state of undress that rivaled that of the most aggressive ladies of delight he'd ever seen on the streets of Brest or wandering through the regiment's winter quarters.

She seemed not to be aware of either her own dishabille or Yves' response to it, and focused on showing them what looked like one solid horse after another. By the time Corporal Braun and the horse seller joined them in the barn, Gerard had commented, "It almost looks as though they preserved a company of horse left behind by the English for our benefit."

Yves cocked an eyebrow at his friend and said, "Then this merchant is making a canny deal indeed—for the cost of a few months' time feeding them, he has gained a set of horses worth many thousands of livres. A sharp dealer, this one."

Gerard laughed aloud at Yves' speculation, earning both of them a pointed glance from the *bas-officier*. Braun and the American spoke in rapid-fire English at one another, until the soldier smiled and the horse seller grimaced, and they shook hands.

Gerard said quietly to Yves, "He has agreed to purchase the lot of the horses the moor showed us, at a price that would buy one a small estate back home." He sighed unhappily. "The deal did not include the two black horses we looked at, though. Corporal Braun does not believe that they will be of use to us, and so he did not even offer a price for them."

Yves said, "As may be, but in the meantime, we have a large number of horses to move down to the hussars' camp. We had best get to work on that, no?"

"Correct," Corporal Braun interjected. "We will take as many as we can now, and come back for the rest." He frowned in the direction of the seller. "He might change his mind. Let us not permit that."

The horse seller had called his slave over and was giving her instructions. She caught Yves looking at her and turned her face away, seeming now to be embarrassed, and Yves immediately felt shame for his wandering gaze.

He turned away, embarrassed that her master would have so little regard for her modesty or comfort as to permit her to be in such a state, and averted his eyes as the horse seller spoke to her in rapid-fire English. As she returned to the barn, he relaxed a bit, but she quickly re-emerged, carrying a large coil of rope.

Braun said, with his typical brevity, "Put leads on at least a dozen. Use what rope you must. We'll each take four." Yves and Gerard nodded and as the two soldiers and the dark-skinned girl passed through the gate into the field, Yves noticed with a flash of irritation that Gerard was eyeing the slave girl with open appreciation for her ragged clothing. As for himself, he kept his gaze steadily on her face as they worked.

He saw that her eyes were dark and lively, and she was quick to smile anytime they were working with a horse that misbehaved in some way. She tied makeshift halters for the horses with deft hands, and as she gave Yves the lead to the first one, he ventured a simple English phrase he'd learned, saying, "Thank you."

She gave him another smile and answered, "*De rien.*" He was too startled to respond immediately, and he simply led the horse over to the fence to tie it up while they finished preparing the others for the brief march back to their encampment.

When he returned, though, he asked her, "*Tu parle français?*"

Without looking up from the rope she was knotting into a halter, she nodded, answering in French, "Yes. My mother came from Africa to Sainte-Lucie, in the Caribbean, but when I came of age, I was sold to a plantation on Guadeloupe, a few islands away. During the passage, our ship was taken by a British privateer, and I was brought here instead." She shrugged. "The work here is easier than what I saw my mother have to do on the plantation where I was born."

Yves opened his mouth to reply, but Braun interrupted. "There's no time for talking," the corporal called out. "Get the rest of those horses ready."

Yves nodded in mute resignation, taking the halter the slave girl handed him over toward the horse the *bas-officier* held ready. Gerard whispered as he passed by, his eyes filled with mirth, "There's no need to sweet talk the wench as though she were a girl from town you were wooing. Just make an arrangement with her master, and take what you want."

Yves' hand acted as though by its own will, and shot up to slap his friend full across the face. Gerard stood, shocked for a moment, and then his hand rose slowly to feel his reddening cheek, his expression disbelieving.

His face storming up, Corporal Braun shouted, "Soldier! Return at once to the encampment; consider yourself under arrest. I will come and deal with you shortly."

Without a word, Yves numbly dropped the halter to the ground, and walked through the gate to comply. He could feel both the slave girl's and Gerard's eyes on him as he departed, and all the way back to the camp, he wondered at the rage he'd felt at Gerard's words. Whatever the consequences, he had no idea of the cause of his sudden act of violence.

Chapter 14

Corporal Braun's massive figure darkened the entranceway to his tent and Yves scrambled to his feet, the fear he'd kept at bay all afternoon rising to consume him whole. The *bas-officier* stood silent, regarding the soldier for a long moment.

"You are very fortunate," Braun said finally. "Your messmate will not demand satisfaction of you. He says that you were playing only, and did not strike him out of malice. Only I and the civilian saw you strike him."

He sniffed heavily, as though something repugnant lay in the air. "You will not face the court-martial. Do not let it happen again. That is all; return to your duties."

The corporal turned on his heel and left, and Yves sat heavily on his bedroll. All of the questions that he had been skirting in his mind came pouring in now.

Where had the rage that had overtaken his reason originated? What about Gerard's jest had so infuriated him? What honor did a slave have to defend, and why had he been moved to defend it?

He shook his head in frustration, as there were no satisfactory answers to any of these questions.

Gerard had not been wrong—though the little town lacked a population of ladies of delight, he had heard other men laughing and joking about having found release with some of the slave women they had found among its residents. The horse seller hardly seemed likely to be a man of such high moral rectitude that he would have been offended or even resistant to a proposal such as Gerard had suggested. Perhaps a little coin—specie was always welcome in a place where the paper currency was worthless almost as soon as the ink dried—or the promise of a future favor, and the arrangement could be made, and without the normal effort involved in winning a girl's heart.

He was spared further self-reflection as Gerard poked his head into the tent, saying, "We're ready to go and get another set of horses, and the corporal wants you to assist."

Yves started to say, "Hey, Gerard, I'm sor—" but the other soldier cut him off.

"Forget about it. It never happened; just a shame that Braun thought he saw you swing at me. It was all just a misunderstanding, right?"

Yves' brow beetled, but he nodded slowly, standing up. "Very well, if that's how it is."

Gerard regarded him steadily. "That's how it is, yes." He turned to leave the tent, and then turned back with a grin. "If you ever want to think about actually taking a poke at me, though, you'll wish that you had only a flogging to fear."

Despite himself, Yves returned his friend's grin. "That seems fair."

Gerard tipped his head and left, and Yves followed him out of the tent and back into the sunshine.

They spent the rest of the afternoon with a couple of other men, marching up to the horse seller's field, gathering up another group of horses, and marching them back to the fortifications, where a much larger squad was engaged in building a stout fence to surround a paddock adequate to the hussar's newly-acquired herd. The slave girl was nowhere in evidence about the barn, but the man who had sold them the horses was present, closely supervising the men to ensure that they gathered up only the horses with which he had agreed to part.

Just out of the man's earshot, Gerard commented at one point to Yves, "It is a pity that he watches us so closely, else I might sneak into the barn and see about that fantastic pair of horses he has in there."

Yves grunted noncommittally and Gerard added, "It is also a pity that we have yet to be paid, so that I might ask you for a loan sufficient to make this fellow an offer on the beasts."

Yves shook his head with a dismissive smile. "You over-estimate my ability to wisely hold onto money myself. If you are so inclined, I suggest that you speak to him and see what terms he might entertain."

"There is no point in that; such fine horses are well beyond my means, and I know it. It is just an idle thought." With that, Gerard bent to the task at hand, and Yves did likewise.

There were still only enough animals to seat about half of the hussar company, but it was an improvement over the pathetic sight of men who were accustomed to drilling on horseback practicing maneuvers on foot. In the days that followed, those troops who did now have horses were fully occupied in training them to French drill—which clearly differed in certain respects from the drill the animals might have previously experienced.

Yves wondered at the monumental waste of war, where an army might casually abandon property worth several lifetimes of an ordinary soldier's pay, and another might almost as casually purchase a like amount of property for no more than a short-term purpose.

Though it had been several days since the incident, Gerard had been true to his word and had made no mention of it. Yves, however, remained keenly aware of the rupture between them, and was still angry when he considered his friend's offhand comment. He was, however, no closer to understanding the reasons for his anger.

One afternoon, after drill was complete, and as they sat in their tent, Gerard got out his dice. "Cast your lot, and see if you can win enough to buy some apples?"

"No, thank you—you know that I don't care so much for games of chance, nor have I the coin to spare at such entertainments. I would rather purchase just a few apples than give you all my pay against the chance that I *might* purchase more apples than I could eat." He smiled at Gerard, who nodded and caught up his dice in his hand and dropped them back into his rucksack.

Henri appeared at the door to their tent, looking quite excited, and said, "You fellows need to come and see this! A delegation of savages has arrived to treat with the general, and they are something you will remember for all of your days."

Gerard, grinning, said, "Well, then you must have a guess that I will not live for so many more days," but he moved to follow Henri.

Yves stood and dusted off his palms on his trousers. "Any diversion is better than sitting here dreaming of home," he said, smiling. He had been considering whether to chance another letter to his mother, given the misfortune that had befallen the last one. "Let us come and see these savages of yours."

The three soldiers joined a curious throng that had gathered at the entrance to their fortification. There, Yves could see some twenty tall men, truly striking in appearance. Rather than trousers and shirts, most were naked from the waist up, the hair of their heads shaved off along the sides, leaving a strip along their crowns, which was plaited into glossy, black braids. They wore belts with some sort of blankets folded over them, draping down their legs to fill the function of trousers, but Yves could see that they were freer to move about than European dress would allow.

One of the men strode forward, and Yves said to Henri, puzzled, "What is that on their feet?"

Henri strained to look more closely, and replied, "Some sort of stockings, it appears, but made of deerskin, perhaps?"

Yves noticed, too, that most of the men seemed to have some sort of rings in their noses—two or three in each nostril, and multiple rings in their ears as well. Some had their earlobes sliced into narrow strips of skin, from which they hung glittering stones. Several of them had tattoos as well, marking their faces and giving them an even more outlandish appearance.

Yves supposed that the Frenchmen, with their high-plumed hats, heavy, colorful jackets, and solid boots, probably looked bizarre in the savages' eyes as well, but he confessed to himself that he preferred the French mode of dress and accoutrement.

General Rochambeau was there to greet the visitors and they were apparently expected, as his adjutants carried gifts, which he presented to the leader of their delegation. When the adjutant gave them a number of royal medallions, Yves was surprised to see the savages kiss them and immediately hang them about their necks, a most auspicious gesture. Their leader distributed among the delegation the white blankets and sabers, along with the other goods the general offered them.

With these preliminaries concluded, the general and his entourage led the savages' delegation back into his headquarters, and the crowd that had gathered to see the spectacle began to disperse.

An officer emerged from the headquarters, though, and called the men to order.

"All units should prepare for parade. We will be offering our guests as many entertainments as we can devise, and the general wishes to begin by giving them a demonstration of our drill and order. After the drill demonstration, we will have a general feast, solemnizing and celebrating our alliance with their nations."

A cheerful "huzzah"—a response adopted lately from their American hosts in the place of their more familiar "*vive le roi!*"—rose in response to this news, and the men dispersed to make themselves ready for the drill demonstration.

The savages stood in a group, accompanied by the regiment's top officers, on a small rise to one side of the fortification, as the men assembled to show off what a modern professional military could do.

Dressed in their finest uniforms, taken from the bottom of their shipping chests, the regiment looked resplendent, though Yves thought that they smelled a little musty at close range. They demonstrated several close-order drills, executed with snap and precision, and then stood stiffly at attention while the grenadiers loaded three rounds of shot, which they fired in rapid and synchronized succession from all of the guns placed around the perimeter of the fortification.

As the smoke from the gunpowder drifted back into the fortification, Yves saw several of the savages grimace and cover their noses at the smell. He'd always found the reek of discharged gunpowder vaguely pleasant, but he supposed that a people who were more accustomed to the woods and rivers might find it offensive to their noses.

From the water, an answering boom of gunfire announced the naval part of the demonstration, and several of the great warships passed in succession under the walls of the encampment, their sails gleaming white in the sunlight, and their pennants flying proudly. As they passed, each of them ran their guns out, though none fired again. They maneuvered smartly to come about and pass again, this time each firing a volley out over the bay, a terrific concussion of noise and smoke.

Once the last ship had passed in review, on its way back to anchor, the troops were dismissed, and after putting away their dress uniforms, the regiment's musicians came forth to play a selection of their favorite dance and martial music, accompanying the meal, which consisted of the cooks' best efforts with a relative wealth of fresh ingredients now available. Puddings containing lavish amounts of spices and meat, delicately-flavored stews of beef and pork, and mounds of bread—some made in their own ovens, and some purchased, though Yves had avoided being assigned that particular duty.

The savages dispersed themselves into the regiment, sitting where they wished and sharing in the meal with great enthusiasm. Only one spoke any English, and he happened to sit with Yves and Gerard, where he and Gerard conversed in a mixture of words and gestures. After a brief exchange, Gerard turned to Yves and explained, "This fellow is named Ginawo, and says that he is a chief among the Skarure tribe, come here through many days of travel. They are most worried about how the English will treat with them, now that they have fought on the behalf of the Americans, and they wanted assurances that we French remain their steadfast allies."

Yves smiled at the man, seeing in his eyes the sort of open friendliness familiar to him from the expressions of any person of good will he'd ever met. There was sadness there, too, and loss. He wished that they shared a common tongue, but he made do with a universal smile, and offered the savage the trencher of stew. The other man laughed and patted his belly, then held up his hand, adding a comment in English.

Gerard smiled and said, "He said to thank you, and that the stew is some of the best he has ever eaten away from his own fort, but he has already eaten so much that his stomach is thinking about bursting."

After the music, a small comedy troupe that had sprung up gave a performance, a routine that centered about their squad's inability to load up a "cannon" fashioned from a hollow log. Though Yves didn't find the performance all that funny, the savages were laughing harder than most anyone in the assemblage, particularly when the ball rolled out of the open end of the mock cannon and fell onto one of the men's feet. Yves winced and hoped that the ball was not real, for that man's sake.

After the meal was over, it was the savages' turn to offer entertainment. When they emerged from the tent that had been provided to them for the purpose, they had dyed their hair in crimson and adorned it with all kinds of feathers. Their skin was also painted red, but they had marked themselves with various decorations in black, consisting of wreaths about their shoulders, scatterings of stars, human figures and other symbols. Altogether, if they had appeared savage on their arrival, now they looked downright otherworldly.

The group of them gathered into a circle and began humming together, shifting from one foot to the other in unison. One of the men had a small drum, which he began to beat in sync with their movements, and their humming swelled in volume, taking on a rhythm of its own, which grew into words shouted in a monotone as the men began to prance around the center of their circle. They continued in this vein, their shouts sometimes shifting to a shrill shriek, then returning to an energetic chant.

They sang, leapt and jumped for as much as an hour, to the point where their sweat was washing the paint from their bodies, leaving the figures they had painted themselves with indistinct and smeared. When they finally came to a stop and fell silent, the regiment sat in silence for a long moment, as though stunned by the energy and savagery of their performance, before they stood and applauded their guests, whistling and stomping in appreciation.

The savages grinned and bowed, and Yves saw Ginawo catch his eye and give him an individual wave of greeting before the delegation retired to their tent to get cleaned up.

Gerard turned to Yves and said, "Well, those are some impressive new allies, are they not?"

Yves was about to answer when another soldier leaned over and said, "You heard about the gifts that they offered the general, did you not?"

Yves and Gerard shook their heads in unison, and the other man grimaced. "Along with some articles of their clothing—those odd soft shoes of theirs, and some belts and other trinkets, they gave him a collection of scalps taken, they said, from English soldiers that they had captured and killed in a great battle."

Gerard's expression mirrored Yves' horror at such a practice, and both of them recoiled visibly from the other man.

Gerard said, "Surely you are mistaken in this. Why, the one with whom I spoke at supper seemed almost a civilized man, even if his English was odder than even my own."

"I did not see the trophies for myself, but that German they brought along assured me that it was a common practice among their people to collect such mementos of their military victories. He has lived among them for a score of years, and is so enamored of them despite their savagery that he told us that he expects to spend the rest of his days among them."

Gerard's eyebrows rose up to disappear into the thicket of hair that fringed his forehead, and the soldier continued, "If they are so savage to the English, what might stop them from doing likewise to any who might be so unfortunate as to fall into their company? He may well spend the rest of his days among them, but those days may be fewer in number than he anticipates."

Yves raised a mollifying hand and said, "It is possible, but I must say that when I looked at our supper companion, I did not see a man dedicated to savagery—at least, no more so than any soldier at war—but I did see a man who would do what it took to protect his hearth and family. Are we so different ourselves?"

The soldier leaned back, saying, "If you find me with parts of any man—even an Englishman—hanging from my belt, you may call me a savage, but until then, I figure that I am their better. In any event, I won't be turning my back on these fellows, and so long as they are here, I'll be sleeping with a knife in my hand."

Yves refrained from rolling his eyes, but he could scarcely believe that the man with whom he had broken bread posed any threat to his safety here.

Gerard smiled and said dismissively, "Friend, you are safer here than you would be in your bed back at home across the sea. Did you see how impressed they were at our parade and naval review? They need our alliance to protect them from the wrath of the English, and you fear that they would also invoke the wrath of France on top of that?"

He clapped the other man on the shoulder. "Now, if you should like something to be truly afraid of, come and join my dice game, and let's see whether you can take my pay or not."

Chapter 15

The grass in the field was as high as Yves' hip, and was dry enough to rustle loudly as he moved through it. He held his musket before him as he walked slowly, half-crouched, trying to move slowly enough that he would make no sound, despite the dry grass. He held his musket at the ready, with the pan primed and the bore packed with an innovative load that the Americans were fond of, consisting of a standard ball, preceded out of the muzzle by several small buckshot pellets.

Gerard had urged him to try the new load, saying, "General Washington insists that all of his troops load this way. They call it 'buck and ball,' and it's said to increase the likelihood of striking your target significantly."

"But can the buckshot stop a target as well as a ball?"

"No, but it's better than a miss, and if, on the other hand, you are a lucky shot, you will strike your target with the entire load, which will drop most anything you might shoot at."

Yves had nodded thoughtfully and had taken a handful of the premade paper cartridges Gerard had offered. Now, out in the field, he had torn the back off one with his teeth, primed the pan, and dropped the rest of the cartridge down the barrel of his musket, following it with the ramrod, which he used to gently tamp the load down firmly into place at the back of his gun's barrel.

His musket was prepared, then, as he saw a rustling in the

grass ahead of him. He did not hear his quarry's telltale sound, but he could now see the grass moving about, perhaps thirty yards away.

Moving very deliberately, he brought the musket to his shoulder and sighted down the barrel at the point at which he anticipated that his target would appear. He took a deep, calming breath, his finger sliding inside the loop that protected the trigger and resting on the fatal bit of metal gently.

As he expected, a group of geese burst up from the ground, taking flight and presenting a multitude of targets, wheeling into the sky. Yves pulled the trigger, and over the deafening roar of the gun firing by his ear, he thought he heard the high-pitched shriek of . . . a girl?

Two of the geese he had fired at faltered and dropped to the ground with distinct thumps. It sounded as though one still had some fight in it, honking and struggling in the grass, but the other made no sound at all. Between Yves and where the birds had fallen, though, a head popped up, dark of hair and skin. The look of utter terror in her eyes made the horse seller's slave girl all but unrecognizable at first. She looked at Yves and the terror on her face gave way to recognition, and her shoulders slumped as she sighed audibly in what sounded to Yves like resignation.

She lifted her hands into the air, tears streaming down her cheeks, and she called out in her oddly-accented French. "Please don't shoot, *monsieur*. I do not want to return to my master, but I want to live, even . . . even if it means going back."

Yves' mind was awhirl with confusion as he realized that he was still holding the butt of his gun to his shoulder. Immediately, he lowered it and slung the weapon back over his shoulder. He called back, holding his own hands up in reassurance, "I did not mean to frighten you; indeed, I did not even know you were there."

She nodded and said, "I was hiding and was not aware of your presence in this field, either, until you shot at me." She glared at him, her dark eyes flashing, and he gasped in disbelief that she could think that he would have fired on her.

"What? I did not shoot at you!" He gestured past her, to where the wounded goose could still be heard struggling. "I am here hunting for my supper only, and did not think that there was another soul in this field."

She began to lower her hands, looking over her shoulder at where the geese had fallen. He could still see the apprehension in her expression as he said, "Let me but put that poor beast out of its misery, and then we shall talk, all right?"

She nodded, but did not move from where her feet were rooted in the field as Yves passed by on his way to the fowl. He could feel her eyes on him, wary and scared, as he walked past.

One goose lay silent, victim of a clean shot through the neck. The other had been struck in the wing, incapacitating it, and the bird hissed and beat at him with its good wing. He closed in on it, disregarding the bruises it was inflicting with its struggles. A quick flash of his blade, and the wounded bird joined its companion in the quietude of death.

Yves turned away from the geese to see the slave girl running in the opposite direction, toward some low, wooded hills. She ran with her hair streaming out behind her where it had escaped from her cap, and for the first time, Yves noticed that she was now clothed in what he might consider "proper" fashion, with what appeared to be a worn, but serviceable apron tied over a relatively new-looking linen shift. He was relieved for her sake, and wondered if her master's improved fortunes with the sale of his horses to the regiment had led to some improvement in her condition.

He sighed and shook his head, turning back to deal with the birds. They would make for a rich meal, a welcome break from the steady diet of corn and the occasional beef. They would also be a heavy load for the long walk back to camp.

When he returned to the encampment with the geese, Gerard was the first to spot him.

"Well, so I see that you've had a successful day. You got two with one shot?"

"Indeed—one very lucky shot." Yves hesitated, then added, "I very nearly got a blackbird with the same shot."

Gerard gave him a quizzical look and said slowly, "Not enough meat to bother with on those, though I suppose that the red feathers are pretty enough."

"No, you miss my meaning. That slave girl from the horse seller—the one that caused us the . . . misunderstanding."

Gerard's eyebrows disappeared under his hairline and stayed up. "You mean to say that you encountered her out in the field where we saw all the geese the other day?"

"That's the very place, yes. What's more, she thought that I meant to shoot her, and lit off for the woods as soon as I turned my back."

"Oh no, that's bad," Gerard said, a look of grave concern coming over his face. "She must have run away from her master."

It was Gerard's turn to hesitate before speaking. "He will probably publish a reward for her immediately. . . it's a pity that you didn't bring her in, for her own safety."

Yves was taken aback. "Assist in capturing a slave? It is bad enough that the brutal institution is so widespread in this country, but for us to act in its defense or preservation in any way is abhorrent."

Gerard held up a hand in a mollifying gesture. "I understand your position, but consider that every farmer and trader in these parts will be looking for her by week's end, when her master's notice appears. She has no legal protection that any of them are obliged to observe, and not everyone has your fine sense of right and wrong."

Yves looked startled, then concerned. "She might come to grief for my failure to persuade her to return to her master?"

Gerard nodded. "It is possible, though you cannot hold yourself responsible for her actions."

Yves swallowed hard, shaking his head. "I did not think about the implications of suffering her to run away from me, as I had the geese to contend with. When she lit off, I just accounted it to distrust of my person, and did not give any consideration to others taking up the chase."

He unslung the geese from his back and handed the carcasses to Gerard. "Here, give these to the cook with my compliments. I hope that he can prepare them more delicately than the last ones he was given."

Gerard looked startled as he took the two heavy birds from Yves. "Why will you not give the geese to the cook yourself?"

Yves gave his friend a grim look. "I need to go find that girl, for her own safety."

Chapter 16

All the while that Yves was making ready to trek into the woods after the girl, Gerard was following him about, attempting to dissuade him.

"You'll miss your next watch," Gerard said as Yves threw bread he had grabbed from the mess tent into his haversack.

"You can cover for me."

Gerard grimaced. "I have duty the watch after yours. You cannot ask me to pull two watches running."

"I'll be back in time to take your watch; so far as the *bas-officiers* need know, we simply traded watches."

Gerard frowned, his forehead deeply furrowed. "It will look as though you plan to desert, and you know that the punishment for that is death."

"I would hardly desert and leave all of my effects behind. I am taking only what is necessary to track the girl and see to her safety."

"Do you mean to return her to her master?"

"I do not." Yves hadn't realized until he spoke that he had no interest in seeing the slave returned to her master, but wanted instead to assist her in making good her escape, and evading any slave hunters that the horse seller might have set on her trail. He cast about the tent, saying as much to himself as to Gerard, "I shall need some canvas for a tent, and an extra haversack." He opened the common chest of the mess's goods along the back wall of the tent and tossed through the items stored within until he found what he sought, and pushed them into his haversack.

Gerard gaped at him. "You have taken leave of your senses. I should report you to a *bas-officier*, for your own good."

Yves scowled at him. "Are you so unmoved by the plight of an innocent girl, afraid for her life, alone in the forest with the prospect men of ill intent in pursuit of her, that you would prevent me from going to her assistance?"

Gerard pursed his lips in a deep frown. Slowly, he said, "No, I am not unmoved, but the ways of the Americans are not ours to pass judgment on. Were we in France, or even in the Indies, I might feel qualified to hold an opinion, and even to take action. But here, where we are present only to assist our hosts in their struggle against the English? It seems to me to be a presumption at best, and at worst, interfering in the dispensation of justice in a sovereign nation."

Yves took a deep breath and answered, "Some values are universal, Gerard. The ownership of one human being by another is repugnant to our souls, and every fiber of my being now cries out to do something about it. When an opportunity such as this presents itself, it is the only path open to me."

Again, he realized he had not given the matter so much conscious thought until challenged to do so, and even though he found Gerard's challenge to him irritating, he was grateful to have cause to clarify his thinking to this degree.

Gerard's frown softened by a minuscule amount. "You sound, my young friend, like a revolutionary yourself." He stepped aside, out of the doorway to the tent, where he had unconsciously moved to block Yves' path. "Good luck to you, and be careful."

"Thank you, Gerard. I'll be back by the end of my watch."

As Yves hurried down the road in the middle of the encampment toward town, Gerard muttered to himself, "I hope that the girl is worth it, *mon ami.*"

After a brisk walk that left him slightly winded, Yves arrived at the edge of the woods, near to where he'd watched the girl disappear. Pausing to catch his breath, he examined the ground for any trace of her passage. Seeing none, he looked around to be sure that he had his bearings; he could just see the trampled grass where he had struggled with the wounded goose. Near where he stood, he recognized the great oak at the spot where the girl had ducked under its lowest branches as she entered the forest.

He hiked the heavily-laden rucksack into a more comfortable position on his shoulder and walked closer to the oak. There, under the low-hanging branch, he saw the print of a stout shoe pressed into a patch of soil where last autumn's leaves had blown clear. Stepping into the woods, he could see disturbed leaves and grass in a clear track. He grinned as he stepped more briskly into the gathering darkness of the forest. It was fortunate for him—and for the girl—that she had no idea of covering the marks of her passage, and that he was the person to find them. He used a fallen branch to obscure the path behind him as he followed the track.

A few dozen paces into the trees, his grin faded as the tracks just . . . stopped. A clear path blazed through the undergrowth, and then it was as if she were plucked up bodily from the Earth.

His brow beetled in consternation, he retraced his steps to see if she had doubled back and then gone some other way, but he could detect no trace of that sort of trickery.

Returning to the end of her tracks, he frowned, and cast his gaze upward—and he saw it. Just the hem of her shift, over the edge of a large branch on an extraordinarily large elm.

He called up to her. "*Madamoiselle*—for shame, I do not know your name!—it is your friend, the soldier who came to purchase horses from your former master. I see you up there, and I am here to help."

He could hear her sharp intake of breath when he first called up to her, but for a long moment, she answered with silence.

Finally, just as he was scoping out the handholds she had used to lift herself into the tree, she called back softly, "Are you alone?"

"Yes."

"My mother named me Amalie, but my master always just called me Philly. It made him laugh to use the same word for me as for his female horses."

He smiled gently and called back, "Then I shall call you Amalie." As Yves spoke, a crack of thunder sounded, followed almost immediately by the sound of heavy raindrops hitting the crown of the forest. "You had better come down, as the lightning likes to strike the tallest objects it can find. Your tree is one of the larger ones in these woods, and I would hate to see it bring you to grief."

She had squeaked in fear with the thunderclap, and now she cried out, "How do you know this to be so?"

"I have heard from another soldier that Doctor Franklin of Philadelphia has made a study of the phenomenon, and indeed, he has even gone so far as to offer a device to channel lightning away from the flammable parts of a house."

He made an impatient sound, adding, "If you wait for me to give you a whole lesson in natural philosophy, you shall be struck dead by the storm before I can reach the conclusion." The rain had begun to filter through the forest crown now, and was dripping heavily from the leaves overhead.

He saw her hem jump out of view as she began to scramble down the branch where she had taken refuge. The deepening darkness of the forest was rent by a flash, almost immediately followed by a tremendous concussion of thunder, and she screamed, dropping from where she was, nearly directly over Yves' head, down to the forest floor at his feet.

She sprang from the ground to clutch at Yves' arm, and he was surprised at how tight her grip was. Instinctively, he wrapped an arm around her to give her some shelter under his cloak from the rain, which was now sheeting down from above in a torrential downpour. Another flash of lightning struck, a bit farther away this time, and he could feel her tremble and start when the thunder struck like a cannon shot. The wind now rose, wailing through the trees overhead.

Putting his mouth near her ear to be heard, he said loudly, "Amalie, give me but a moment, and I will erect a shelter for us. Take my cloak—it will keep you dry, and will only hinder me."

She nodded, and he slipped the garment from his shoulders onto hers. She clutched it about herself, and he gave her a comforting smile, and then began digging through the haversack for the canvas he had filched from the chest in his tent.

Working quickly, he set up a rudimentary shelter, making use of some fallen trees nearby, and the length of rope he had also stashed in the haversack for the purpose. Amalie watched, rainwater streaming from her cap and down over the cloak. He could see that she was becoming drenched, and he realized that the rain was soaking through his own clothing. He needed to get them under cover, and soon, in order that they would not catch their deaths of cold.

Once he had the canvas secured, he ducked down to sit on the ground under it and called to the girl. "Come under here, and we shall have some shelter from the storm."

She nodded, looking miserable, and joined him in the close confines under the canvas. They were shielded from the worst of the wind, though an occasional gust would blow raindrops into the open face of the shelter.

Amalie huddled close to him, and he could feel her shivering already, as the rain and wind combined to steal her warmth. He was feeling the effects of the wind even with his heavier garments, and he could only guess how much of the wind was penetrating the linen of her shift.

Assuring himself that it was only for the warmth necessary to ensure her survival, he pulled her close to him under his arm and stroked her back briskly for a while to provide some additional warming. She sat, shivering, her chin tucked into her chest, until she began snoring softly, her form relaxing into his side. Even as thunder pealed and rain poured from overhead, she did not stir, and eventually he began to relax as well.

All through the night, the storm continued to rage overhead, but the little sanctuary they had found felt like a tiny bubble of peace and safety in a world gone to madness and thunder.

Chapter 17

Yves awoke with a start as Amalie shifted under his arm. The thunder, which had been a constant backdrop to his troubled dreams, had rumbled off into some other district, though rain continued to pour through the canopy of the forest overhead. Though he could hear the wind moving through the trees, it was no longer so strong as to blow under their shelter. Without the flashes of lightning, he could scarcely make out his even his feet in the darkness, much less see anything outside of the shelter.

His back and shoulder screamed for relief from the awkward—yet strangely comforting—position in which he'd slept, half-way leaning against the girl, and half-way embracing her. She was warm under his arm, and he couldn't help but notice how bony her shoulder was under his hand.

She stirred again, turning to face into his chest, her breath warm against his neck. He absently stroked her hair, and she murmured something in her sleep that he could not make out. He froze and moved his hand back to her shoulder, shaking his head at himself over the unintentionally familiar gesture.

Yves pursed his mouth in the darkness as he tried to think of what he would do in the morning. He had already broken his commitment to Gerard to return for the next watch, and come the sunrise, he would be marked as absent from the rolls. If he was not seen by the following muster, he would be marked as "deserted," and the only welcome he could expect would be the raising of a gallows upon which he would be suffered to dance.

And, in truth, did he owe more to his *bas-officiers* or to the distant King himself than he did to the girl beside him? They would succeed or fail no differently with him among their ranks than in his absence.

Too, what future lay before him, if he faithfully returned, abandoning Amalie to find her own fate? Uncertain service, indifferent superiors, and the likelihood of death, whether by miserable, lingering disease like Luc or by the more merciful instrument of an enemy's shot.

By joining her, he could find some different fate, in a land where whatever king reigned was at a reassuringly safe distance. He realized as he pondered that he already felt certain of the ultimate futility of the American cause—the unwelcoming townsfolk, the threat of English ships and patrols, and the miserable condition of the town had all conspired to convince him—and that he did not particularly want to share in its coming defeat.

It seemed as though the die were cast already, and only one path remained open to him—and to Amalie.

He was hindered by many factors; chief among them was language. Amalie spoke both English and French, though, which helped. Too, he was penniless, and he expected that she was likewise. Finally, he knew little of the lay of this land, though it was possible that Amalie had some destination in mind when she had flown. He was unarmed, but their safety lay in remaining undetected by any possible pursuers rather than in fighting.

His mind was still buzzing with plans and potentialities as he drifted back off to sleep.

When he awoke again, birdsong and the first rays of morning sunlight greeted him. He'd slumped into a prone position in the night, the rucksack under his head, and Amalie was draped halfway across his chest, still slumbering peacefully. A rock had found its way between his shoulder blades, but he was loath to disturb her, so he willed himself to ignore it.

He studied her face in the morning light, her features relaxed and soft. He had never had the opportunity to look this closely at a moor, and he found that there was an unfamiliar beauty to her face. Her lashes were as long and as delicate as any girl's he'd ever seen, and her dark brow was smooth, unmarked by her waking worries. The whorl of her ear was a wonder of gentle curves and slopes, and if her nose was broader than his own, it suited her well.

A branch cracked nearby under the weight of some forest creature, and her eyes flew open. She gave a small, stifled shriek and sat up, pulling away from him.

"I beg your pardon, *monsieur*," she said, huddling to herself. "I did not realize that I had fallen over onto you in the night."

He held up a hand in a gesture of reassurance. "There was no harm in it, Amalie."

Sitting up, he winced at the knot in his back where the rock had dug in. "Well, perhaps a little harm." He stretched his neck and reached back to massage the painful spot. Taking a deep breath and shaking his head sharply to dispel the pain, he turned and brought forth the rucksack.

"Would you like some bread to break your fast?"

Her eyes widened and she nodded. "I have not eaten since yesterday morning when I—" She broke off and bit her lip.

He brought out a loaf of the bread and tore half of it off,

holding it out to her. She looked at it, but did not move, her eyes wide and fearful. "When you ran away," he said gently. "Here, take it."

She reached out and accepted the bread from his hand, but before she ate from it, she said quietly, "How much of a bounty will you earn from my master?"

He gaped at her, then said, "I did not seek you out to capture you, Amalie. I came to preserve you from those who would hunt you. Now, my service in the regiment is forfeit, and we must run." He took a bite of bread and after he'd swallowed, added, "Together."

It was her turn to look at him with a disbelieving expression. "Wherever will we go?"

He gave her a half-smile and said, "I had hoped that you already had a destination in mind. I had planned to conduct you there, and then make my way into the countryside, to find some community where I could make a home." With a sudden pang, he realized that he would likely never see his own home again.

His face filled with pain, and he said brusquely, "Eat. We need to be moving before too many people are about."

He focused on chewing and swallowing, though the bread was now dry and tasteless in his mouth. He could not help but think of how differently it was made than what his mother had raised him on, and he was abashed to feel a tear make its way down his cheek.

He shook his head forcefully, as if to drive away the emotions that had overcome him, and took a deep breath, pushing down his feelings in order to deal with the challenges that stood before him.

Amalie did not inquire into what was troubling him, but

instead followed his command, at first eating as mechanically as he was, and then eating with real eagerness as the first bites awakened her hunger.

He finished his half of the loaf first and stood, brushing his hands off on his trousers. The canvas that had shielded them held a deep pocket of water in one corner, and he reached to push it over the side, but then thought better of it. Walking around to the outside, he cupped his hands and brought a double handful to his mouth, drinking gratefully.

Once his thirst was slaked, he asked, "Do you want some water before I tip it out of the canvas, so that I can dry and fold it?"

She nodded eagerly, stuffing the last bit of bread into her mouth and standing. Once she had drunk her fill, he poured the rest of the rainwater over the side and began untying the canvas. As heavy as the winds had been, he was surprised and pleased at how well the makeshift shelter had worked.

As he folded the canvas, shaking it off to get rid of as much water as possible, Amalie said quietly, "I have heard that certain of the folk in town, who are called Quakers, may help a runaway slave to find safe passage to a distant community, where none will pursue."

Yves continued folding, absorbing what she had said thoughtfully. "Do you know where any of these Quakers might be found?"

"I do not . . . I had never thought to escape until"—she gave him a pained look, then pressed on—"until yesterday morning."

Yves did not pry. He knew that slaveholders sometimes indulged in excesses against their servants, and he found that he did not wish to know the details of Amalie's impetus to her sudden decision to flee.

"I do not think it wise for either of us to be seen about town. We will do better in a place where our faces are not known to anyone." He considered for a moment, pulling the spare haversack out of his own, and pushing the canvas into it to keep it separate from the dry things he carried. "Do you know the roads out of town well?"

She shook her head. "I don't know them at all. Ever since I was sold here, I have only ever traveled from the farm to the village on my mast—my former master's business." She smiled in spite of herself. "I do like the sound of that, 'former master.'" Yves returned her smile, and offered her the haversack with the canvas in it.

They set off together, retracing her path through the field where he'd encountered her the day before, and then swinging along with the Sun at their backs, staying off of established roads. Wherever possible, they skirted woodlands, so that they could duck into the cover of trees if they spotted anyone.

Yves saw that the storm had taken down branches in many places, and had even uprooted a few trees along their path. He was grateful for not having suffered any falling limbs or trees hitting their shelter the prior night.

As they walked, Yves asked Amalie about her childhood in the Indies. "An old friend of mine once told me that it was only good for two things—rum and biting flies of various diverse sorts." He smiled, and then saw a look of mild irritation cross her face.

"My *maman* and *papa* worked in the cane fields, farming the sugarcane used for that rum, until they both became ill and died within a fortnight of one another. As for biting flies, I used to lie awake at night, scratching at the welts that they raised on my legs and arms. I would continue until they bled, or until my *maman* came and held me in her lap until I slept." She looked at him with a wistful smile and added shyly, "I dreamt last night that I was again in her lap, but when I woke up, it was only you."

He gave her a smile in return. "I am glad that you had the opportunity to visit your mother in your dreams."

"As am I, *monsieur*." She smiled and gazed into the distance as they walked, lost in thought.

Yves considered telling her to simply use his name, but decided that it was not in keeping with the story they had agreed upon, that if they encountered anyone, they would pose as master and slave, traveling together for an unspecified purpose. He was uncomfortable with the fact that the ruse would require him to take on the persona of a person who claimed ownership of another human being, but it was the only plausible story they could think of. It had the advantage of being all too believable.

Around midday, they came upon an isolated farmhouse with a tidy little barn beside it. From the edge of the woods, they observed the farm for a long span before concluding that its proprietor must be away on some business that left his property unattended. Seeing chickens running about, Yves said to Amalie, "Though we have yet another loaf of bread, I wouldn't mind some eggs, if we could find where they are laying."

Amalie nodded avidly, and together they crept forward, alert for any human presence. Yves slipped into the barn with Amalie close behind him, and gave a triumphant smile as he spied the nest in the corner with several eggs clustered together in its hollow.

He bent to pick up his prize, but froze as a voice came from the dark corner of the barn, saying, "Thou art welcome to some eggs, but I would prefer that thou ask before taking."

Chapter 18

Yves did not understand what the farmer had said to him, but the man's gravely calm voice somehow felt more menacing than an overtly angry tone. He stood up from reaching toward the eggs, moving slowly and deliberately, and holding his hands in clear sight, just in case.

Amalie hissed into his ear, "He speaks in the manner of the Quakers."

His heart sank as he realized that they had made the worst possible first impression on a man who might well have been the key to their salvation. Worse, it seemed likely that he would share with his co-religionists that first impression, crushing their chances of seeking aid from that quarter at all.

Willing his breathing to remain calm and collected, he said, "Please tell him that we're sorry for trying to steal from him, and that we want no trouble."

She translated, her voice quavering slightly, and the man stepped out of the shadowed corner of the barn.

He was dressed eccentrically, wearing plain, sturdy clothes instead of the fashionable, ornamented clothing Yves had seen other Americans wear, and not just on Sundays. His face was broad and impassive, his eyes active and alert. He, too, seemed to be moving with care, and keeping his empty hands in view.

He answered Amalie, and then asked her a question and in

her response, Yves heard her give their names. He nodded, satisfied, and as she continued to speak, her words sounding to Yves as though they were rushed and fearful, the farmer moved toward the barn door, motioning for them to follow.

He reached the doorway and stopped suddenly, clearly having heard something in Amalie's torrent of speech that had caught his attention. He asked a short question, and she answered.

Yves saw the grimace on the man's face and suffered a moment of doubt that he feared would bring his heart to a standstill.

The farmer seemed to come to some momentous decision, though, as he sighed deeply and shook his head in apparent resignation.

He said something else, and Amalie finally translated, "He says he will help us to hide and escape."

Yves felt a wave of relief wash over him, almost as though he were on the deck of a ship sailing through summer heat, caught by a chance splash of cool ocean water.

She and the farmer conversed again briefly, and then he left, and she explained to Yves, "He is compelled by his faith to assist us both—I, because I have been held in bondage, and you, because you seek to escape warfare and violence."

Yves objected, "I did not depart for being shy of battle, but only out of concern for your welfare!"

Amalie gave him a surprised look, though her expression swiftly shifted to being guarded and wary, before she resumed her explanation. "He said to wait here, while he explains matters to his wife, and makes arrangements to conduct us from this place to another, further away from the town, and those who might recognize and apprehend us."

A sudden thought struck Yves and he asked, "What is he called?"

"He introduced himself as simply Benjamin, and would not suffer me to call him even *monsieur.*" She frowned, as though she did not fully believe the farmer's words as she reflected upon them. "He said that all men are treated as equals before God, and it is only proper that we treat each other as equals in this life."

She leaned toward him, as though to confide in him some shocking secret, and added, "It sounds as though I am not the first escaped slave that he has heard of being assisted by those of his faith. I am surprised that I have never heard of such a thing from the other slaves I know here about the town." She frowned. "Perhaps they thought that I was not trustworthy enough to share with me such a secret as a way out of bondage."

Yves said, reasonably, "Or, perhaps they never knew. What slave in your position would take the risk to go back now and give word to friends that their salvation might be open to them—at the risk of his own?"

She nodded slowly. "I would not, and I am not even that well known by my face around the town."

Yves found that hard to believe, as he found her face quite memorable, but he kept his counsel. "How long are we to stay in the barn, then?"

"He did not say, but it sounded as though we would leave with him under the cover of darkness."

"Isn't that running the risk of encountering a French or rebel patrol—or worse yet, English forces skulking about the countryside?"

She shrugged. "He knows these parts better than either you

or I. We shall have to put our trust in him."

Yves sighed. He preferred to have more control over his destiny, but fate decreed otherwise on this day, it seemed. He opened the flap of his rucksack and pulled out the last two loaves of pilfered bread. "Hungry?"

Amalie nodded with enthusiasm, and he handed over a whole loaf. The two of them were still tearing off chunks of bread and chewing when the farmer returned.

He was carrying bedding tucked under one arm and a small pot of steaming soup in the other hand. He smiled to see them eating bread, and Yves saw for the first time that he had deep crow's feet emanating from the corners of his eyes, betraying a long life of habitual smiles. Though his clothing was plain, and his faith austere, he was clearly a man who found deep joy in life.

He offered the bedding to Yves, motioning with his chin to place it in the same dark corner from which he had surprised them earlier. Yves took the blankets and hurried over where he was directed, finding a clear spot in the shadows to put them down.

Setting the small kettle of soup down on the wide, clean-swept planks of the barn floor, Benjamin spoke to Yves and waited patiently for Amalie to translate for him.

"He says that he expects that we did not sleep well last night, and he can see that we have not supped adequately, and so he brought some of their meal out to share with us. He would have invited us into the house, he said, but they have a four-year-old son, and children of that age are incapable of seeing something and not later speaking of it freely."

Her brow beetled and she added quietly, "At least, I have been told that is the case."

Shaking her head to dispel the sadness that had fallen over her, she said, "He tells me that it is plain, but nourishing, and will go along nicely with the remains of our bread."

Yves smiled at Benjamin, saying, "You are truly generous and kind, and I cannot conceive of any way in which we can ever repay you."

Amalie conveyed what he had said, and Benjamin returned Yves' smile gently and spoke. Amalie, her eyes filled with wonder, translated, "You cannot repay me. What you can do, however, is to look for an opportunity to assist someone else in the future, as I have assisted you. When you do so, you will have repaid me fully, and I will know that your debt to me has helped some other person who found himself in a spot where he had to rely on the goodness of strangers. Today, it is my turn to be that good stranger; in time, you will find your turn."

Yves grinned and said, "Tell him that I will repay him many times over, with gratitude and joy."

Amalie conveyed the message, and he replied briefly before leaving to return to the house. "He said that he is already repaid then, and that we should enjoy the soup with a clear conscience."

With a smile, she sat before the soup and dipped the end of her bread into the kettle. "You had best join me, else I will have to eat all of this without you."

Chapter 19

"**H**e says that the first leg of our journey is the most perilous, *monsieur*." Amalie was translating again for Benjamin, as they both ate good bread, spread thickly with sweet butter, while a barn cat wound about their ankles, voicing occasional demanding yowls.

Yves tossed the cat a corner of the bread, frowned and said, "I would prefer that you not call me 'sir.' My name is Yves, and I should think that it is good enough for you to utter."

Amalie gave him an odd half-smile and said quietly, "You have been listening too much to Benjamin, with his ideas of all people's equality before his God."

Their host and benefactor had woken the pair early in the morning, before daybreak. He had loaned them bedding to make up two separate spots in the hay, and they had fallen asleep separated by an arm's length. Yves had awoken to Amalie's head cradled on his chest again, though, and Benjamin had looked away after waking them, a smile twitching at the side of his mouth. He now busied himself with a wagon on the far side of the barn.

Yves had jumped up and volunteered to assist Benjamin with whatever he was planning, but the farmer had shooed him back to eat the breakfast he had brought out.

Amalie continued relating Benjamin's explanation of his plan. "We will be obliged to conceal ourselves under the cargo he will load into the wagon, and we will take passage on the ferry off the island, over to Bristol.."

Yves looked up sharply. "There is no bridge from here? I knew not that we were so thoroughly hemmed in by the geography of this place, and had thought to simply cross under darkness, and trust any guard to be lax and weary."

Amalie looked abashed as she answered, "I had not yet devised a way to cross over the ferry, and before we happened into our friend's good graces, I was working up the courage to inform you of that aspect of our predicament."

Yves waved away her concerned expression. "The problem is now out of our hands, and in our host's capable ones. It is no longer of any consequence, in any event."

She nodded, still uncertain, and continued. "Once we cross the ferry, we will need to travel for several more hours, and then Benjamin will commend us to the care of a friend of his whom he believes will be kindly disposed to assist us."

Yves smiled. "I do hope that our good fortune continues."

"As do I, *monsieur.*" He shook his head slightly, but was not bothered enough to correct her. He remembered Henri's dismissive phrase, "Don't call me sir—I work for a living," but decided that it didn't sufficiently apply to him at this time. What was he but a deserter and an unemployed soldier? He had no profession outside of soldiering, and now had no position within it.

He sighed, and Amalie, mistaking it for a continuation of his earlier request, gave him a playful smile. "As you wish, Yves." It was the first time she had said his name, and he found that he liked the sound of it.

Benjamin called to them, and Amalie said, "He has our

hiding place prepared." More quietly, she added, "One might think that this was not the first time that he had smuggled someone off this island."

Yves did not answer, but was looking skeptically at the space that Benjamin had prepared for them to secret themselves within. It was in the narrow span between the wheels, and was only as long as the distance between its axles, which looked to be not quite a man's height. It was in a portion of the bed of the wagon that apparently had a false bottom with a shallow box that was concealed from the outside as part of the framework of the wagon's body.

"We are to both fit within there?"

Amalie craned to look over the side of the wagon herself at the space provided, and conveyed the question to Benjamin.

The farmer answered with a grin, and Amalie said, "He tells me that this space has concealed two full-grown farmhands who were avoiding their duties, so he believes that we will be able to make do, at least until after the ferry."

Yves gave a resigned shake of his head and climbed up into the wagon. Reaching down to take Amalie's hand, he helped her up behind him, and together they stepped down into the compartment.

It was deeper and longer than it had looked from outside, and Yves sighed, lowering himself into the space. Amalie followed, and after they had sorted out where elbows and knees needed to fit together, he found himself spooned in front of her, with her breath tickling the back of his neck.

Benjamin looked over the side of the wagon and nodded approvingly. He made a comment, and Amalie whispered, almost directly into Yves' ear, "He says to relax now and stay calm, as he must cover us up. There will be plenty of air, but not very much light, so long as we are not detected."

Yves nodded silently, and Benjamin swung himself over the side of the wagon, making the whole thing rock slightly. He reached back over the side and lifted up a section of the flooring of the wagon, which he carefully fitted over the two huddled figures. Once he had them enclosed, he brought in his horse and hitched it, and then drove the wagon out to the field to load a small stack of hay into the bed of the wagon.

Climbing back into the driver's seat, he clicked at his horse and directed it to draw the loaded wagon out of the field and onto the narrow road that led to the ferry.

There, he paid the ferryman for the crossing and waited for the vessel to return from the far side. He ignored the small squad of French soldiers on guard duty at the crossing, nearly refusing to acknowledge their warlike presence, as usual.

Within the secret compartment, Yves had long since gotten over the novelty of having the young woman's body prone against the length of his back, and was far more aware of the awkward angle he had been forced to adopt for his arms, and where the boards underneath them pressed uncomfortably into his hip and ankle.

The morning had been a cool one, but in the close space, he was starting to sweat, increasing his discomfort. In addition, he was becoming keenly aware that it had been too long since either one of them had had a chance to bathe, and the atmosphere in small space made him highly self-conscious.

The only consolation was the soft sensation of Amalie's arm, where it had crept around him as the only outward sign of the terror that the girl was experiencing.

They had bounced and rocked over the roads, and now, as they waited in the stillness for the ferry, Yves found that the dust raised by all of the motion had gotten into his nose. He snaked his hand upward to pinch the bridge of his nose, trying to forestall a fatal sneeze, a noise that would betray their hiding place and bring disaster to them all.

He felt the urge pass, but behind him, he felt Amalie's body stiffen with a sudden, explosive sneeze of her own. Just at that moment, though, Benjamin shifted about on the seat, causing the entire wagon to rock, with a multitude of small squeaks and creaks, covering the modest small noise of the girl's sneeze.

After a moment, when it was apparent that they had escaped detection, Yves dared to breath again, and he felt her relax against his back as well.

Shortly, they began to jolt forward again, rolling onto the noisy, hollow sound of the ferry's deck. The noise abated as Benjamin set the brake on the wagon, and then the familiar sensation of moving over water replaced the jolting of rolling over roads for a short while.

Soon enough, though, Yves heard Benjamin thank the ferry pilot, and the wagon jerked back into motion.

Incredibly, he heard Amalie begin to snore softly into his ear, and even more incredibly, he found himself drifting off to an uneasy sleep as well, rocked into complacency by the unceasing motion of the wagon, and into exhaustion by the tension of the passage.

After what felt like some months of constant travel, Yves returned to wakefulness at the sensation of the wagon turning carefully off the road and down a small hill, and then coming to a stop.

Amalie began to stir behind him as he heard the farmer moving around over their heads, clearing off the cargo he had used to conceal them. The farmer called out to someone in the distance, sounding both tired and exultant.

A few moments later, Benjamin lifted the false bottom off the pair of fugitives, and they both raised their arms in unison to shield their eyes from the bright noonday Sun.

The farmer reached down and offered Yves his hand. Yves accepted it and arose shakily from the compartment. Benjamin helped the girl up in turn, and then assisted them both out of the wagon.

As they climbed down, an older man, dressed in similar fashion to Benjamin, approached the wagon, surprise etched on his face at their appearance from under a load of hay. He said nothing, though, and the two Quakers walked away a short distance had a brief, intense conversation. Yves saw the old Quaker nodding rapidly as Benjamin spoke, his expression thoughtful and approving.

Finally, the two returned to the wagon, and the old man held up his hand in greeting, saying something that Amalie translated sleepily, "He says, welcome to freedom. We have escaped from the island."

Chapter 20

Benjamin took his leave, shaking the reins and giving his horse a quiet command. The animal was reluctant to leave behind the sweet grass in the field, but it slowly pulled Benjamin's wagon back up to the road. Within minutes, he had disappeared around a bend in the road, leaving Yves and Amalie alone in the company of the elderly Quaker.

"Where will we go next?" Yves felt lost in the wake of Benjamin's departure, in addition to being stiff, sore, and disoriented from the wagon ride.

Amalie, looking a bit forlorn herself, answered, "Thomas has agreed to house us until we determine what destination should suit us best."

At mention of his name, the old Quaker offered a quick grin, and said something to Amalie, then gestured for them both to follow him as he went back into his house.

Amalie started off in Thomas' trail, and Yves followed and said peevishly, "I suppose that I shall have to learn English if I want to understand anything that's being said to me from now on."

Amalie did not answer him directly, but said over her shoulder, a trace of irritation in her own voice, "He said only that we should follow him for a meal and some fresh clothing." She seemed about to add something more, but she restrained herself, which almost irritated Yves more than an argumentative answer might have. Having a runaway slave girl show him how to exhibit grace and self-control was not an experience he had ever expected.

He shook his head and trudged along behind the old man and the girl up to the house. When they entered, they found a tidy, comfortable living space, but one that had evidently been home to only the one old man for some time.

A hint of sadness in his eyes, he conducted them up narrow stairs to a pair of bedrooms on each side of the massive chimney that rose through the upper floor of the house. He said, and Amalie hastily translated, "These were once used by my son and daughter. They are gone, but I've kept their rooms as they left them. There are clothes on the shelves that you may use." He directed Yves to one room and Amalie to the other, then went back downstairs.

As he was changing into the plain linen shirt and brown trousers he found in the shelves, Yves heard Amalie call out through the wall, "Yves?"

"Yes, Amalie?"

She sounded almost shy as she said, "I had to learn English when I was sold to my former master, so I understand your frustration. If you like, I . . . I could teach you."

He nodded, and then, realizing that she could not see the gesture, called back, "I should like that very much, Amalie." He hesitated, and then added, "Thank you."

Yves finished dressing, pleased to find that the clothes fit him reasonably well, though the trousers were a bit shorter than he might ordinarily have worn. He brushed the caked-on dirt and straw from his boots and put them back, however, as the shoes that were in the room were impossibly small.

Amalie emerged from her room, wearing a sturdy-looking

green dress. Yves noticed that although she had changed into a fresh shift, without mud about the hem, she had also kept her old shoes. She had donned a modest bonnet, covering her hay-laden hair, and had a cloak over her shoulders.

He nodded and smiled. "You look as neat as a pin. That dress suits you, better than these trousers do me."

She smiled shyly. "These are the finest clothes I have ever worn, nicer even that what my *maman* could provide me when I was little."

To his surprise, he saw that Amalie's eyes had welled up at the mention of her mother and her childhood. Instinctively, he drew her into an embrace, patting her back to comfort her. Her hand went to his shoulder and she sniffled just once, resting her head on his shoulder.

For his part, Yves was keenly aware that his mother, too, was as distant from him now as if she were in her grave, and he suppressed the tears that threatened to well up again in his own eyes.

Thomas called up the stairs and she startled, pushing away from Yves. She replied to him, and then said quietly to Yves, "I'm sorry, I just . . . I miss my *maman*, and wish I could ask her advice now." Yves understood, he thought, better than she might know. She indicated the stairs with her chin and added, "Thomas has food waiting for us."

At the table, she maintained a cheerful conversation with their new host, translating for Yves throughout. They ate another simple soup and bread, though not so fine as had graced Benjamin's table. As he ate, Yves wondered idly to himself if there was some religious command within the Quaker faith that required dependence on soup.

Their conversation avoided the difficult questions for now—how had Thomas come to live alone, why were Amalie and Yves on the run, and what would tomorrow bring—in favor of discussions about the storm that had just passed and the status of the war.

Thomas explained that, since his faith forbade him to participate in violence of any sort, he was no party to either side in the war, but that he nonetheless followed the news of it closely. When the English had passed through the area as they retreated from the island the prior year, an officer had come to demand provisions from him.

"I gave them three pigs, which was more than I could spare, but they were not satisfied," Amalie relayed. "They seized my last cow as well, and said that I was lucky that they didn't fire the place."

Thomas shrugged when Yves asked, "Does your faith not permit you to resist when such injustice is visited upon you?"

"Would resistance have stopped the English from taking what they wanted?" He shook his head. "I know the answer to that already. It would have cost me my home, and possibly my life; and it would have cost the two of you the shelter you now enjoy."

Amalie added something to him, and translated herself, "I told him that we are grateful for his forbearance."

Yves smiled and said, "Indeed."

He frowned and asked, "Have you any word of English troops now in these parts, or do the Americans hold the region uncontested, now that we French have established our fortifications on the island?"

Amalie translated and Thomas laughed aloud, and made

just a brief comment in reply. "The only English who might venture here are spies, and they do not share their plans or whereabouts with me."

He reached up behind himself and held out a pair of apples, saying through Amalie, "Here. Enjoy these while I finish my work for the day, and then we shall all retire for the night. You've had a hard day, and I suspect that you both should like some sleep."

He rose from the table, collected their bowls, and went outside, whistling as he went.

Yves bit into his apple and said to Amalie, "He's right about being exhausted. Even though I slept in the wagon, I feel as though I've spent the day building entrenchments."

She smiled and said, "I have never built entrenchments, but I have spent a day cleaning a barn that had housed too many horses for too long, and I was less tired after that than I feel now." She frowned and sighed wearily. "The first night after I arrived here, when *monsieur* Mason bought me, I might have been more tired."

"Tell me about that?"

She hesitated, and Yves worried that he had gone too far by asking. Then she took a deep breath, nodding, and said in a small voice, "Nobody has ever asked me about it before, but I have dreams about it many nights."

She regarded him steadily, her expression serious. "Are you certain that you want to hear this story? It is not a pleasant thing to contemplate telling it, nor do I expect that it will be pleasant to hear about it."

Yves nodded, unsure of the motivation that drove him to know all about this episode in Amalie's past, but unwilling to back away now.

Again, Amalie took a deep breath, then began. "It was before the war began, and, as I told you, when I came of age, I was sold away to a plantation on Guadeloupe. The plantation where I was born had too many slaves, and so the *econome* chose some of us to go."

She got a faraway, almost wistful look in her eye as she continued. "Before then, the routine was always the same: Up at sunrise with the horn, prayers and roll call, and then out to the field, where I and other children followed behind the first two crews, each of us carrying a basket. We would pick weeds out from between the canes when the fields were growing, and pick up the loose leaves and scraps during the harvest."

Yves nodded. His own childhood had included simple chores about the farm such as these, though he had little doubt that his father had been a far easier taskmaster than the *econome* on the plantation of Amalie's childhood.

"After a few hours, it was time for breakfast, which sometimes my *maman* cooked, and after she was gone, another woman. Then we'd go and work cleaning around the mill, or in a different field, until midday."

She smiled, saying, "That was the only time we got to play, although sometimes we had to sit and wait for our driver to inspect our feet for chigoes, to ensure that we would not be lamed in our work."

Yves gave her a puzzled look. "Chigoes? What is that?"

"They are tiny bugs that bite into the bottoms of your feet, and cause a swelling. When my friends got them, they were hardly able to walk until they healed, and even after, they said that they could feel where the bites had been."

Yves nodded, understanding visible on his face. "Ah, you mean the *aoûtat*. We have them in France as well, although they are mainly something that your *maman* warns you about to remind you to wear shoes outside."

Amalie smiled gently. "We had no shoes, nor any clothing to speak of. It was too hot to wear much when we were working, and the *econome* never saw the point in giving us anything to wear anyway."

Yves blushed and changed the subject. "What did you do after your noonday break?" He turned and spat seeds from his apple out into his palm, and went back to eating it.

She laughed and said, "Why, we went back to the fields, of course. During the harvest, we would work right past dark, seeing by great torches the *econome* would have lit at the edges of the field. The rest of the year, though, we would work until it was dark, and then have an evening meal and go to sleep as early as we could."

She looked down at the floor then, sadly, and continued her story. "One morning, during the roll, the *econome* had several of us stay behind. I had just been moved from the *enfants panier* to the second crew, where I was responsible for some of the heavier work in the fields—we were planting new canes at the time—and I thought that, perhaps, I was being moved to the indoor crew, as my *maman* was before she died, and I was very excited at the prospect."

She looked Yves in the eye with an earnest expression. "You must understand that working in the big house meant being out of the sun, away from the chigoes, and, while one does not get to rest any more than when one is in the fields, the work is at least less arduous."

Yves nodded and said, "It is something like the difference between building fortifications and performing regular drill, in the army."

She smiled quickly. "Exactly. So as I said, I was excited to be held behind by the *econome*. However, my hopes were dashed when a man I did not know lined us up and put manacles on our wrists and ran a rope through them all, so that he could lead us by himself." Her eyes welled up and she said, "I did not even have the chance to visit the place where my *maman* was put to rest, and I never saw the plantation where I was born again."

Steeling herself, she wiped away the tears fiercely and continued. "After that, we were loaded onto a ship and chained to benches on the deck. I overheard someone saying that we were bound for Guadeloupe, and the man who took me from the plantation told the *econome* of the ship—"

Yves interrupted. "The captain?"

She nodded. "Yes, that's what they called him. He told the captain that he wanted us there within three days, since he didn't want to miss the auction there." She made a grim face. "We missed the auction, of course, as we were set upon by an English privateer almost as soon as the hills of our island were out of sight."

Yves nodded. "I have seen an English privateer in action. Though"—he smiled—"that ship was in flight, and not pursuit."

"I should like to have seen that, rather than what I did see." She returned his smile, and went on with her story. "The crew of the ship we were on saw the English ship's sails first, and they began to race about, raising more sails on our ship and distributing weapons of all sorts amongst themselves. They gave no thought to us, though we were exposed on the deck, but were most concerned for their own safety."

She shuddered at the memory. "We were going so fast that it seemed that we were outrunning the wind itself, but still it was not enough. The privateer drew close, and I could see the smoke from a big gun that it fired from the front of the ship. We were not hit by the shot that they fired, but we saw it bounce off the water to one side of our ship."

She shrugged. "As soon as he saw that the pirates could hit us if they so desired, our captain shouted out an order for all of the men to lay down their arms, and he went and pulled down the flag."

She shrugged. "So, there was no battle to speak of, but the real struggle was just beginning. After the privateer's ship caught up with ours, they took our crew prisoner and manned the ship with their own people. Those men moved us all belowdecks together, prisoners and slaves alike. It was even worse than being on top, because the air down there was much worse than it was out in the open, and it was hardly any cooler than it had been out on the deck." Her nose wrinkled in recollection, and Yves' wrinkled in sympathy.

"We sailed for much more than three days, of course. I did not understand anything that the pirates were saying, of course, but I heard some of the original crew speaking, and they said that the pirates could get a lot more money for their cargo—the slaves, he meant—at a place called Newport than they could at any other place along the way. There was something about them being known already in a place called Charles Town, and someone said that he'd heard them say that they knew people in Newport as well."

She shrugged. "It mattered little to us, save that our former masters now shared our fate for a while, confined in irons below decks. At some point, they were hauled out and taken away; we did not know what happened to them, but we did not see them again."

She sighed. "We sailed for a fortnight, maybe longer, and I watched two girls die within an hour of each other. They just laid on the benches, their chains rattling with the motion of the ship. All of us who remained alive cried out as one, and the pirates came down to haul their corpses away. About once a day, they fed us something, and after the girls died, they brought us all up on deck for a little while each day." Amalie shook her head violently, as though to shake away the horror of the memory.

She took a deep breath and blew it out gustily. She spoke quickly now, almost tonelessly, as though to express the emotions she felt about this part of her story would overwhelm her. "We arrived at Newport, and we were moved to quarters at the port there; the next day, we went up for sale."

Yves stopped chewing his apple and could scarcely breathe, so filled with horror was he at the vividness of her account.

"The slave seller brought us up onto a sort of platform, around which there were gathered many men. He proceeded to speak very, very quickly, almost singing, and pointing at one person in the crowd after another and shouting at them. When it was my turn to go up, he made me drop what clothing I had, and I stood naked before all those men. Some of them looked at me a lot, and others seemed bored."

Yves had heard men of the regiment describe going to watch slave auctions in the Indies, but he had never heard so much detail, nor had he ever considered what it felt like to be atop the auction block, rather than simply present in the crowd. He reached out and put his hand on Amalie's shoulder, and she placed her own atop his, smiling briefly in gratitude.

"*Monsieur* Mason was one of the men at whom the seller shouted as I stood there, and in the end, he pointed to my new master, and *monsieur* Mason handed over some coins and took me home." She shrugged. "I learned how to care for horses, and how to speak English. Then the war started, and the English were here. My master stole their horses when they left, and then sold them to you, and now you know my life." She smiled at him. "May I know yours?"

He grinned. "Certainly, although there is not so much to tell. I grew up on a farm with my *maman* and *papa*, until he died and left my brothers and I to take care of the everything."

He shrugged. "I joined the army to provide some income in hard currency to the family. With the start of the war, and the farm's proximity to my regiment's winter quarters, they have been able to sell enough to the army to be less dependent on my salary . . . which is a good thing, since deserters don't get paid."

He frowned, adding, "I only hope that I have the opportunity to explain to my *maman* just why I had to leave."

"I have heard *monsieur* Mason speak of posting letters to what friends he still has in England, so I should think that you can post a letter to your *maman*."

"Oh, certainly, though it was easier when I was still in the army. I sent one letter, but watched the loss of the boat carrying it and the general's dispatches. If I am to send another I will have to find someone to write it for me, and someone to sneak it into the next packet to France."

He shrugged. Inconveniences such as this were part of the price to be paid for his decision. He had had plenty of time to ponder and enumerate them all during that long night in the storm, and expected that he would, with time, come to peace with the trade-offs.

With a start, he realized that the storm had been only two nights before—but what days had intervened! He was about to comment on it when the front door to the house flew open and Thomas stepped inside, closing it firmly behind himself.

The old Quaker looked visibly shaken. He addressed Amalie urgently.

Amalie looked alarmed as she answered, and downright terrified at his response. Yves asked urgently, "What is the matter?"

"My old master, *monsieur* Mason, has posted the reward for my return, and some men have come to ask the Quakers in the area if they have seen me. He intends to spend whatever it takes to have me returned to his service!"

Chapter 21

Yves' mind exploded with questions, but he took a deep breath and asked just one. "Are they aware that you are here?"

Amalie had a quick conversation with Thomas, and then answered, "A pair of them came by to speak with Thomas, as they said that all Quakers are suspect when a slave escapes." She gave a quick, uncertain smile. "I cannot imagine why that might be."

"Are we in danger of being discovered at this moment?"

"No, he said that the men left, but he expects that they and more will be on watch." She shuddered. "I have heard other slaves in town speak of the relentlessness of those who seek the bounty for a captured slave, but I never dreamed that *monsieur* Mason would set a reward high enough for them to bother with me."

Yves said, with a grim expression, "He is newly wealthy, with the money he made selling to the regiment all of the horses he stole from the English. He must have felt it worthwhile to make the example of you."

Amalie looked down at the floor for a moment, then looked Yves in the eye and said, "Perhaps I should just give myself up then, take the whipping I've earned, and spare Benjamin, Thomas, and you the trouble that I have brought upon you all."

Yves' blood ran cold, and he said forcefully, "You will do no such thing, if for no other reason than that my life is already forfeit as a deserter, so your sacrifice would be for nothing."

Her eyes widened and she clutched at Yves' shoulder. "I had no idea, my dear friend, that you had risked so much by coming to my assistance!"

He placed a hand over hers, shook his head, and smiled. "The life of the army is in warfare, and once the bullets begin to fly, none are safe. Aiding your escape is as likely to have saved my life as to cost it."

She smiled, but her eyes still looked unhappy. He squeezed her hand and released it.

He said, "Does Thomas need us to flee then, to spare him the possibility of being charged with some criminal act related to concealing us?"

Amalie posed the question to Thomas, and the old Quaker's expression seemed offended at the question. He answered, his words tumbling over one another like waves piling up on the shore, and when he fell silent, he motioned toward Yves, as though to command her to provide him with a translation.

She frowned and did as he bade her. "Thomas says that he will never bow down before the tyranny of the slave master, and indeed, he will insist upon accompanying us to a place of safety— after we have had a good rest here. As many days as we need, before we travel."

Yves' eyebrows went up and he said, "Please assure him that I meant no offense with my question. I was merely concerned for his safety, and Benjamin's, as I am unfamiliar with the laws here regarding the assistance of runaway slaves."

She relayed this clarification, and the old Quaker's reply. "He will look after his own safety, and Benjamin took the necessary steps to see to the security of his family and farm by bringing us here."

Thomas added several more comments, in the course of which Amalie gasped and put her hands to her face. Finally, with tears welling up, she explained, "As for himself, he says that he has nothing here worth remarking on left to lose. His wife and two children were drowned in the process of going over to Newport last year. They were rowing a small boat—a skiff?—across to the island when a sudden storm came up, and their boat was overturned into the bay. Only his wife's corpse was ever found, and though he says that he had hoped to sleep beside her someday, he finds now that even that cold comfort is unappealing to him."

Yves closed his eyes briefly and said a prayer for the spirits of the dead, then looked at Thomas' face, which was resolute and calm. The older man appeared to have come to some decision, and the outlines of it seemed monstrous to Yves.

"What of his farm?"

Amalie relayed the question and the answer. "He says that it was forest when he started, and it will go back to forest when he is gone. He has no son to leave it for, nor a daughter for whom he might pledge it as a dowry. It's just him and the few animals that the English did not take to feed their army, and that the next passing army will likely take even those."

"But where will he lead us? Does he know the parts distant enough from here to be secure from those who pursue us?"

This question led to an extended conversation between Thomas and Amalie. She related the outlines of it to Yves. "While he has not traveled as much as some he knows, he has faith in the inherent goodness of the people of this country. He has the wit to elude English patrols—or French, now—and his faith gives him certain customary protections from either. Those protections, of course, do not extend to us."

"Will we have to travel concealed, as we came here?"

Thomas laughed as she repeated the question for him. "He says that Benjamin has a certain flair for the dramatic, and while some concealment may be necessary from time to time, he does not anticipate that it will be anywhere nearly so uncomfortable as what we endured to get here."

Yves smiled, saying, "I wondered whether we would really be sought so avidly as to require such measures, but I believed that he knew better than I the risks of traveling over the ferry. Indeed, had we been detected there, you would doubtless already be back under your former master's control, and I would be readying myself for a meeting with the hangman. I shall not scoff at Benjamin's dramatics."

"Nor will I," agreed Amalie gravely.

"How far does he anticipate taking us?"

Thomas shrugged in answer to the question. Amalie translated his reply, "As far as it takes for us to be in a place where we need worry no more about reward seekers or French soldiers."

Yves looked about the neat kitchen, everything in it clearly put in its place as soon as its sole user was finished with it, and all the cooking implements obviously well cared-for. The wide hearth, a small fire crackling merrily in it, with the pot containing the remnants of their soup hanging from a crane, seemed impossible for this man to leave behind, even for the duration of just a trip of a few days.

Yves found himself overwhelmed with a sudden wave of

homesickness, and he wondered how his mother fared. She would not yet have gotten word of his desertion, but she was worrying about him nonetheless for the lack of certainty as to his fate.

"Will he need to make arrangements for the care of his farm, minor though it may be?"

Amalie relayed the question, and frowned at the answer. She asked another sharp question, and he answered with a single word and a serene smile.

Her frown deepened to a scowl. "I believe that he means to leave everything here behind him, and to start anew wherever our fates may lead us."

Chapter 22

The sun shone brightly through the trees, and a pleasant breeze carried the salt-spray smell of the ocean even as far inland as the old Quaker's farm as the little party set out on their journey.

Thomas had spent the time between announcing his decision to Yves and Amalie and their departure in packing rucksacks full of as much food as he could muster—the animals of the farm would not be abandoned—and what gear and clothing he thought might be of use to them on a trip of indeterminate length, with an indefinite destination.

Yves asked Amalie, "Are you comfortable with the bags as they are loaded on you?"

With a flash of irritation in her tone, she answered, "Do you think that I am unused to carrying heavy loads? Just because I am not built like a great ox of a man doesn't mean that I cannot bear my share of our burdens." She shook her head and held up her hands apologetically. "I am sorry. I am consumed with worry at the road ahead of us, and I did not sleep soundly last night."

He nodded and said only, "It seems a waste to have spent your last night under this solid roof for some time *not* sleeping."

She snorted. "You certainly slept deeply enough, if your snores are any gauge of your rest." She delivered the rebuke with a smile, though, and he returned it, glad to see her natural good humor return.

Thomas said something to her, and she nodded to him as she answered. Their host hiked his rucksacks into a more comfortable position and started out toward the road, not even so much as looking back.

Yves had seen him the previous evening, kneeling beside his wife's carefully-tended grave at the edge of the woods. The man had not been praying, as far as Yves could tell, but was merely *being* there, near to the final resting place that he had anticipated for himself, and never for his wife.

Yves had not interrupted his host, but he could not help but watch the Quaker for a few minutes. He was unclear as to the spiritual elements of the other man's faith, but he could see clearly that it brought peace to what could only have been a moment of deep turmoil. For that, Yves was envious.

The turmoil in his own heart seemed only to be growing with each passing day. Used to a daily routine, bound by the requirements of his service, he found the relaxed pace of the farm put him on edge in a manner that he could not clearly describe. For years, he had risen, mustered with his company, eaten his meals, performed his assigned duties, and returned to sleep according to the demands of someone else's schedule.

Here during the precious few days between their arrival at the farm and their departure from it, Thomas left both Amalie and Yves to their own devices, even refusing their help most of the times that they offered it.

The road worn but even beneath his feet, Yves' fingers worried at the worn rosary his mother had pressed into his hands as he'd left, but even repeating the well-graven words of comfort and reassurance under his breath did little to quiet his mind. "*Ave Maria, gratia plena, Dominus tecum. Benedicta tu in mulieribus, et benedictus fructus ventris tui, Jesus. Sancta Maria, Mater Dei, ora pro nobis peccatoribus, nunc, et in hora mortis nostrae. Amen.*" He was halfway into the second decade of the cycle when he heard over his own voice the distinctive sound of a party of horsemen behind them on the road.

He called out urgently, but quietly, to Amalie, who was a few paces ahead of him. "Quickly—we must conceal ourselves!" Thomas heard Yves' tone and cocked his head, hearing the hoofbeats himself. The three of them hustled into the undergrowth, and had barely come to a standstill when the first members of the party swung into view.

Yves' heart nearly stopped dead in his chest as he saw Corporal Braun, resplendent in full uniform, leading a small company of guards. Yves was further surprised to see that they were escorting both General de Rochambeau and Admiral de Ternay, who were discussing something trivial, looking comparatively at ease on their horses. Although he had—thankfully!—never yet had a personal interaction with either man, he recognized them both from the drill parades and occasional sightings from a distance at the encampment.

Ironically, this was the closest he had ever seen either man. Rochambeau looked weary but determined, and Yves had sometimes thought that, noble blood aside, the man had something of the look of his father, a certain gentle resolve about his eyes. The Admiral looked, to Yves' eyes, frankly unwell. He was sweating heavily, though the temperature was quite comfortable, and his eyes looked sunken. It was hard for Yves to believe that this diminished man was the same who had led the fleet ably to safety on these shores.

Braun was, typically, stiffly upright in his saddle, his eyes alert for any hint of an ambush or danger. Yves barely breathed, praying silently that he and Amalie and Thomas were well-enough concealed to escape the man's detection. *In Nomine Patris, et Filii, et Spiritus Sancti . . .*

The horsemen were not on a mission to seek anyone along the path, however, but were clearly simply in transit—perhaps for a conference to coordinate between the military leaderships—and just happened by a misfortune to pass through on the same route that the fugitives had chosen. In contrast, by good fortune, the horsemen passed without incident, and Yves began breathing again.

It struck him then that it was somehow upside-down that he and Amalie feared for their safety and liberty from those who had ostensibly been sent here to fight for the safety and liberty of the American rebels. He shook his head, dismissing the thought.

In hushed tones, Thomas asked Amalie something, and she relayed the question to Yves. "Will there be anyone following behind, do you think, or are we safe to return to the road?"

Yves had never been part of an escort, as that was a duty of the hussars, but he didn't remember ever seeing escorts trailing the main body of the company, so he said, "I believe we will be safe to resume our journey." He frowned. "I do wish, however, that there were some other path than the same roads that soldiers and bounty hunters might use."

Amalie shuddered slightly, but they had discussed the risks of her being seen on the road, and Thomas, who had helped others evade those who hunted them in the past, did not believe that they were likely to lay a trap of any sort, even for quarry that they were pursuing as avidly as Amalie. In the end, there was little choice, though, as the woods were frequently thick with undergrowth, and all but impassable . . . save but by the roads.

She answered Thomas, who nodded and stood up from where they had crouched. He made a remark as they moved back through the brush to the road, which Amalie passed along. "He says that once we get a little further away from the island, we can travel more openly, with you posing as my master, as we discussed."

This had been a subject of another argument, one that had ranged far into the night. Yves and Thomas were both opposed, while Amalie insisted that it was the only arrangement that did not raise more questions than they could answer to casual observers. It had been an odd sort of argument, as she gave voice to her own opinion in both English and French, while translating the opposing opinions of the two men, who, though language divided them, were united in their positions.

"I cannot pose as Thomas' slave, nor even his servant, as Quakers are notorious for their opposition to slavery, and, unless I am mistaken, they do not commonly keep servants, either. Nor have I any papers to provide evidence of manumission, which I would need in order to travel as a free negro."

Thomas had spoken, and she translated, "He concedes that Quakers have not kept slaves for some decades, and that their view of the inherent equality of all people makes even servants unusual. He suggests, however, that you could falsify a manumission, as though you had once been my master, but had freed me, and I then chose to remain in your service of my own will."

Yves shook his head. "I do not know the proper language for a manumission, even in French, and what's more, I do not write much more than to make my mark."

She nodded agreement, interjecting, "Even if you could surmount those objections, the next document that would be demanded of me would be the bill of sale that clearly established that you did have the right to grant me my freedom." She relayed these arguments to Thomas, who looked stubborn, and made another remark.

Amalie did not quite repress a roll of her eyes. "Now he objects that no good Quaker would even countenance traveling in the company of a man who would hold a slave in bondage."

She answered him, and then restated her answer in French for Yves' benefit. "I told him that he may pass the hours of our journey in discussing with you the evils of the institution of slavery, and argue for my freedom whenever any fellow traveler might be within earshot."

"He would not have to argue very much to win my agreement," Yves muttered. He pursed his lips unhappily. "I think hardly any better of the institution of slavery than does Thomas, you know. What I have witnessed here of it, and the tales you have told me of your enslavement, and your family's, all persuade me that it is an arrangement that is corrosive to the souls of both the master and the slave."

She gave him a quick smile. "*Monsieur* Mason's soul did not require much corrosion, and mine is made of sterner stuff than that. Though it seems strange and distasteful to you, I can relate to you that I have seen free negroes who were not as well provided for at their own hands as they might have been at a master's."

She shuddered and added, "However, it is true that most slaves are treated with less regard than you might give a prize steer, or a good dog. I do not argue for the institution, only for the necessity of *appearing* to adhere to its forms while we travel."

After giving Thomas a summary of where the argument stood with Yves, she turned back to him, smiled almost coquettishly and added, "Besides, I trust that you would be a gentler and kinder master than *monsieur* Mason ever was."

Yves flushed and dismissed the notion with a vigorous gesture of his hands. "I shall be no master to anyone, least of all you, when I have sacrificed so much for your freedom."

Amalie grew suddenly serious and said quietly, "I should not jest about this, I know, and I hope that you can forgive me for making light of it."

Yves made the same dismissive gesture again. "I am not so disturbed by it as that. I know only that I am barely capable of being the master of my own destiny, much less that of another human being."

He looked over at Thomas, who looked defeated and stone-faced. "Has our host any other alternatives to offer, or are we truly left only with this distasteful ruse?"

She asked Thomas, and he shook his head. Yves nodded reluctantly, saying, "So shall we do, then. No papers will be required in the ordinary course of things, and Thomas can help me to learn the rudiments of English by haranguing me whenever others are about."

For now, though, as they regained the road and resumed their march, they walked in silence, each of them shaken by the near encounter with the company of men who could have so easily brought them to disaster. Braun would have identified Yves as a deserter, and Rochambeau had already demonstrated his willingness to order the execution of deserters who were recaptured. Amalie's status in Yves and Thomas' company would not have withstood scrutiny, and the whole trip would have been over before it even properly got started.

Yves inhaled forcefully and blew his breath out gustily to dispel his anxiety over events that had not come to pass. The road ahead was now clear, the sky bright, the air sweet, and their future at least held the possibility of success.

Chapter 23

Yves blinked slowly as the morning light hit his eyes. He sat up with a start in surprise at the unfamiliar surroundings in which he found himself. For one thing, he slept in a comfortable bed in a warm, snug room, with the light that had awoken him passing through a glass window. Outside, he could hear the sound of horse's hooves on cobbles, and the voices of early morning commerce in a bustling town. Through a thin wall, he could hear soft snores that he recognized at once as Amalie's, and the sound soothed his worries.

Gradually, as he awakened more fully, he remembered where they were, and how they had come to be here. At the end of their first day on the road, Thomas and Yves had made camp, and after their evening meal, the three travelers sat around the small campfire Yves had built, talking about where they ought to try to go.

Yves, almost completely innocent of the geography and local information of the area, deferred to Amalie. "Surely you have traveled for your master, or heard from your peers about town about places that might be friendly to a free negro?"

She shook her head. "Free negros are one thing; runaway slaves are quite another. Running away is a thing spoken of in whispers, and only when no master may be within earshot. For the most part, I was never party to a discussion that touched on such details."

Thomas asked a brief question, and Amalie nodded, explaining to Yves that the old Quaker wanted to offer a suggestion. Thomas spoke at some length, with Amalie sometimes nodding encouragement, and sometimes frowning and asking for clarifications.

Finally, she turned back to Yves. "He knows of a man in Providence, which is just another day's walk to the west. He says that this man is well-known in the Quaker community for his opposition to slavery, and for his willingness to provide aid to those who wish to escape from it."

She frowned and added, "Going to see him will involve going into Providence, which is about the same size as Newport, but with the advantage that we are quite unlikely to become known to any of our pursuers there." She shrugged. "I suppose that I am just uncomfortable being in any town, even though I may be convinced that my worry is not entirely rational."

"What does he suppose that this man can do for us?"

"At the very least, he can give us a safe place to stay, out of the hazards of sleeping in the countryside, dodging every patrol that comes by on the roads where we are. He may also be able to suggest some destinations where I may live without fear of being captured, as well as the resources and contacts to reach those places."

"That sounds quite hopeful, actually. It is far better than wandering aimlessly through the countryside."

She nodded slowly. "The risk is simply that this friend of Thomas' is another who is likely to be examined by any fortune hunter who may have seen notice of *monsieur* Mason's reward so far away as Providence."

Yves shrugged in a broad Gallic gesture of fatefulness.

"Thomas navigated such a challenge without difficulty and kept us safe, though it would have been far easier for him to have given us over to the slave catchers. I have little doubt that his friend can do likewise. I am in favor of making the attempt to contact him and to ask for his assistance."

Amalie pondered for a moment, and then nodded again, her mouth pinched into a grimace. "I agree, and I acknowledge that every day we spend on the road is another day where we are exposed to the chance of detection and capture through design or mishap."

When Amalie relayed their discussion to Thomas, the older man smiled in gratitude for Yves' acknowledgment of his management of the slave catchers, and then stood, brushed his hands off, and said through Amalie, "Let us sleep now, that we may rise and finish this portion of our travels well-rested."

The next day had dawned chilly but clear, and the little group of travelers had packed up their encampment quickly, eager to take to the road and whatever fortune fate might hold for them in Providence.

By mid-day, they were encountering other travelers on the road, and though Yves cringed inwardly whenever a passer-by seemed to take more than a casual interest in them, no unfriendly face greeted them, and no pursuer appeared.

Amalie had resumed the outfit she had departed in, as all three of them agreed that even the plain dress that had belonged to Thomas' daughter was fine enough to raise questions if worn by a slave. She had donned the Quaker-style cap and cape over the dress, though, for the practical reason that it helped to conceal her face, and indeed, someone approaching from behind them would be unaware that she was even anything but an ordinary member of a small party of traveling Quakers.

"*Amis*," Amalie had translated Thomas' gentle correction, when he'd heard Yves use the term "Quaker."

"They prefer to call themselves the Society of Friends." She'd smiled and added, "And, indeed, so we are, three friends, traveling together."

As they passed into the town proper, Yves' tension rose ever-higher. Though there were but a couple of slave catchers looking for Amalie, it was entirely possible that any of dozens of men from the regiment with whom he had served might be here on one errand or another—and being recognized and reported by any of them would be a catastrophe.

He had not been able to relax and enjoy the simple pleasures of the sight of a tidy little colonial town, laid out along neatly-cobbled roads and bustling with activity. The departure of the English, and the arrival of the French, had clearly been better for Providence than for Newport. The wharves served a small fleet of fishing and cargo ships, and an immense church stood at the top of the main street in the town.

Unlike Newport, here there were no homes or shops gutted by flame, or simply abandoned to nature. He realized that these symptoms of decline had made it feel as though the entire American rebellion were teetering on the brink of collapse, whereas this town made it feel like it were bursting with enthusiasm and opportunity. As he had, perforce, now joined the American experiment, he was glad to see these hopeful signs of its success.

Thomas stopped at a bakery and asked for directions to the home of the man whom he sought, and as Yves and Amalie stood in the doorway waiting, he thought back to the bakery in Newport. In contrast to the shrewish woman behind the counter there, here a prosperous-looking, busy man dusted flour from his hands to greet Thomas. Instead of a skinny urchin menacing them with a make-believe musket, there was a chubby baby sitting behind the counter, contentedly gumming a crust of bread.

Thomas, having gotten from the baker the information he needed, asked Amalie a question, which she translated for Yves. "Do you see anything in particular that you want from here? Thomas is offering to buy us bread."

Yves' mouth watered at the prospect of bread baked freshly by someone who actually knew his craft, instead of by a soldier indifferent to the quality of his work, or bread baked a day before and snatched in a crime of opportunity. "Just a plain loaf would be most welcome," he said, smiling with gratitude.

Thomas nodded and completed the transaction, handing the baker some of the paper currency the rebellious Americans used. The baker accepted them with a rueful smile, and Amalie whispered to Yves, "We might have gotten a better price with actual coin, but nobody except the French have that to trade with around here, since the war began."

Thomas handed each of them a loaf of warm bread, and set off down the cobbles, a happy smile on his face. Yves and Amalie hurried to follow him up the hill to a modest-looking, but exceptionally well-kept house nearby the church. At the door, Thomas waited for them to catch their breaths and tuck away the remnants of their bread within their rucksacks, and then knocked firmly.

After a scurry of activity audible from within, a pleasant

woman, dressed in severe Quaker garb, opened the door. Thomas introduced himself, and then Yves and Amalie, and evidently asked after the master of the house. The woman nodded vigorously and motioned them all inside. She led them to a comfortable room with a fire crackling merrily in the hearth, and a number of sturdy chairs arranged about the hearth as though to invite conversation.

Amalie said to Yves, "She says to have a seat, and she'll go and fetch her husband."

Thomas took the chair nearest the fire, holding his hands before him to warm them, and Yves sat beside him. Amalie took the next seat, and Yves could hear her sigh with relief at getting off her feet.

As they warmed up, she scooted her chair nearer to his and looked shyly at him up through her eyelashes, her expression betraying her nervousness. Thomas glanced over and then looked away, a small private smile on his face.

When their host arrived, Yves jumped to his feet out of force of habit. The man was energetic and distinguished-looking, and though he was dressed in the plain fashion of the Friends, his unadorned clothes somehow seemed richer than the finest officer's uniform Yves had ever seen.

"Sit down, my friend," the man said in heavily-accented, but grammatical French, continuing in English to greet Thomas and Amalie as he sat down facing them.

He and Thomas spoke with one another at length, while Amalie and Yves sat quietly.

Finally, the man nodded, spread his hands, and turned to Amalie. He spoke to her, and then turned and said to Yves, "My name is Moses, and I will be honored to aid you."

Chapter 24

They had talked long into the night, and Yves learned a great deal about their host and his fascination with—and deep involvement in—local history. Moses had, as a matter of courtesy, shared his stories in both English for Thomas and Amalie, and in French for Yves. He explained that he had learned the language many years ago, as a matter of business need.

"I come from a family of brothers, each of us deeply engaged in the business of this area. It happened before your arrival here, of course, but perhaps you have heard something of the sinking of the *Gaspee?*"

Both Thomas and Amalie shook their heads in negation, followed by Yves when Moses repeated the question for him.

"Well, I will come to that, but first let me begin by describing the path that brought me into the light of the Society of Friends, and the reason for my dedication to the cause of ridding this country of the terrible institution of slavery."

He paused and steepled his fingers before his face for a moment. His expression became somber, and he began.

"Many years before the current troubles began, my brothers and I were in business together as merchants, trading all manner of goods, and we were persuaded that we ought to try our hand at trading in slaves from Africa." Amalie's lips compressed into a tight line, though she said nothing.

Moses acknowledged her reaction, however, nodding and saying, "I could make excuses and say that it was a long time ago, and the trade seemed both lucrative and just at the time, but the plain fact of the matter is that I and my brothers were more concerned with the money to be made than with the moral aspects of the matter. I have suffered decades of guilt for my part in this matter, please allow me to assure you."

Amalie nodded, her mouth relaxing a fraction, though Yves could see that her eyes were still tightened with anger.

Thomas continued his story, though, his tone still apologetic. "We fitted out a brig named the *Sally*, and loaded her with trade goods of various sorts, such as we had been advised by those with experience in the trade would be the most useful in securing a good cargo of slaves at the James Fort on the African coast."

He sighed. "We appointed a man from these parts named Esek Hopkins, whom we knew from prior engagements from the port here, to be the captain of the brig. Sadly, he was largely ignorant of the operation of a slave ship, which brought the enterprise to a disastrous end."

He turned to Yves, adding, "You may have heard of Hopkins as the commander in chief of the American naval fleet, though he was relieved of those duties a couple of years ago, and returned here, where he serves with some distinction in our legislative assembly today."

Yves shook his head, saying, "No, though I have not had much exposure to the American Navy; my entire sailing experience has been with a little French privateer, which bore me hence just a few months ago." He grimaced.

Moses smiled in understanding. "It must not have been very

pleasant." Yves shrugged, having gained some perspective on how easy his passage had been from hearing Amalie's tale of her voyage aboard the privateer.

He glanced over at Amalie. "You have been on a slave ship, have you not?"

She nodded tightly.

Gently, he asked, "And how many were lost on your passage?"

"Two girls, who succumbed to fever and poor food." The anger was back in her eyes, Yves noticed.

Moses continued mournfully, "Esek contrived to lose more than half of the slaves that he transported from Africa. Some, he lost to disease, others to suicide, and quite a few to an insurrection which they felt was their only opportunity by which to regain their freedom."

His eyes bright with grief and sorrow, he concluded, "All together, over one hundred souls were lost on the altar of a base, mean financial trade. At one point, we had gotten word that the ship and all hands had been lost; I truly believe that it would have been better had that news turned out to be true. As it is, I daily seek the light of forgiveness my savior promises, and have dedicated much of my life to ending this trade forever."

He turned to Amalie, whose expression was stunned at Moses' revelation. "In addition to this work, I am also called to provide whatever assistance I can to those who have escaped the chains of slavery, in some small token of compensation for the lives lost. I can never bring back those hundred dead men and women, but I can help to bring freedom to many hundreds more such as you, Amalie."

She nodded, her expression still grim. "I do not know if forgiveness is mine to offer, nor do I know if it will be yours to earn. That will need to be between you and your God. However, I will accept your help, with gratitude that this disaster changed your heart."

Moses closed his eyes and nodded. When he reopened them, he said, "I appreciate the opportunity to assist you."

Just then, his wife bustled into the room and spoke to her husband. He replied to her and stood up. "Our dinner is ready, my friends. Will you join me?"

Already seated at the table were Moses' children, a modest young woman and a bright-eyed little boy. By an unspoken agreement, they did not discuss the slave trade any further during their meal, though Yves noticed that Amalie ate without enthusiasm, as she still pondered the terrible revelations their host had shared with them.

Yves could not help but eat heartily—the meal was plain, as he had grown accustomed to in the company of the Society of Friends, but it was rich and plentiful, and he better understood their host's prosperous girth on seeing how his table was laid.

After their meal, Thomas asked Moses something and he replied, adding in French, "I did promise to tell you the story of the *Gaspee* as well, did I not?"

He smiled. "I am a student of history. I collect all sorts of papers and accounts, but I am also careful to set down the accounts of events that I know well myself, that future generations may learn of them and benefit from studying our errors."

Leaning back in his chair until it creaked and groaned, he began his story. "Seven years back now, there was a British customs schooner named the *Gaspee* that patrolled these waters"— he motioned out through the front window toward the harbor— "looking for smugglers who might have been trying to evade the duties that the English had recently imposed upon our trade. Naturally, my family's ships frequently passed through these waters, and for some reason, the captain of the *Gaspee*, one Duddington by name, seemed to take particular delight in targeting our ships for search and harassment."

He shook his head, a small smile on his lips. "Not that we had any history of smuggling. I had served on a committee that spoke out against the Stamp Act some years before this, and so we were regarded with suspicion, and Duddington seemed to believe that it was his mission to inconvenience anyone who was associated with that opposition as a means of quelling future dissent."

Thomas frowned and asked a question. Moses nodded and said, "Thomas wants to know whether my brothers and I had acted on that opposition, other than in my writing against the Act. The *Gaspee* and her captain sometimes found irregularities in our accounts, and Duddington was fond of seizing ships on the lightest of pretenses, sending them away to be condemned as prizes for the Customs Service."

He smiled grimly. "In fact, he was not able to come ashore here in Rhode Island, for fear of being arrested on warrants that our local magistrate issued against him for his abuse of his powers."

Moses opened his hands as though revealing a secret. "Suffice to say that there was no love lost between the local merchants and the men of the *Gaspee*. So, when we heard from a hastily-docked packet that that the *Gaspee* had run aground while pursuing her, there was a lot of talk about what the merchants ought to do."

He shrugged. "My brother and some other men went out that night in small boats, and approached the ship to see how badly aground she was. You have to understand that not only were they personally affronted by the harassment from the *Gaspee*, but they were also part of the political opposition to the same Stamp Act that I had spoken out against. In any event, whether it was an accident or a misunderstanding, one of the men aboard those boats fired on the ship and struck Duddington."

Grimacing, he said, "We did everything we could for the man and he survived, but he made nothing but trouble for us in the days to follow. He demanded the arrest of my brother and several other men, and wanted them all charged with treason. Worse yet, he wanted them hauled over to England for trial, which would almost certainly would have ended in their hangings there."

He gave a sly grin and added, "Sadly, the commission that they appointed to investigate the whole affair was unable to assemble enough solid evidence to justify bringing charges against anyone, so the destruction of the *Gaspee* was without consequence for my brother."

He got a faraway look in his eye and added, "It may be, though, that history records the burning of the *Gaspee*, and the shot fired at Duddington, as being the opening salvo of this revolution against England. People in Boston and Williamsburg were so alarmed at the prospect that they began coordinating their efforts against the Stamp Act and other Parliamentary actions across the colonies . . . and that led to the formation of the Continental Congress, and that to the Declaration of Independence and our present war against England."

Although the children looked bored, Moses' wife was

paying attention, and Thomas, Yves, and Amalie were all rapt and sat in silence, absorbing what he had said.

His wife spoke up first, and Amalie translated quietly for Yves. "I, for one, am proud to be attached to such a distinguished family, and one so closely associated with the urge for independence, which can only increase the freedom experienced by all peoples in the world. Once we have established the principal that no king may impose his will upon his subjects without their consent, it is but a short step to the principal that no man may impose his will upon his neighbors without their consent, either, thus ending slavery for ever after."

She looked triumphant at the prospect, and her husband smiled indulgently at her. "We shall see whether that comes to pass, my darling. First, we must bear witness to the outcome of the present war. Far be it from me to sound in favor of warfare, but I will go so far as to drink to the health of the Congress, and to the wellbeing and success of General Washington."

Thomas looked uncomfortable with following the English tradition, or perhaps it was the sentiment that kept his cup low to the table, but everyone else raised theirs well overhead and huzzahed, even the children.

Chapter 25

Now, though, it was morning, and the high words of the prior evening were faded into a general sense that they were in the home of a man of great influence, which gave Yves a great deal of hope for the immediate future, and relieved his sense of a pressing need to find a place of safety for Amalie and himself.

Yves lay back in the bed, pulling the warm blankets up to his chin and listening to Amalie snoring softly in the next room. Had it really been less than a week since she had made her fateful decision to run away, and he had decided in a snap to assist her? It didn't seem possible that in so short a time he should have become accustomed to the sound of her sleeping nearby, or the look on her face when she was delighted by something.

He was still pondering these imponderables when he heard footsteps coming up the stairs. Moses' son, who had a peculiar-sounding (at least in Yves' opinion) name, Obidiah, stuck his head into the room where Yves lay. He said something in English and gestured for Yves to come downstairs.

Yves nodded and smiled at the boy, who next went to Amalie's door to rap upon it and also summon her downstairs. Yves heard the girl's sleepy reply and smiled as Obidiah raced back downstairs. He pulled on his trousers and buttoned up his shirt, considering that sufficient for breakfast en famile. He debated waiting for Amalie, but decided against it, heading downstairs alone.

At the table, he found Moses and his daughter engaged in an animated conversation with Thomas, but since his English was still confined primarily to what would be useful in a tavern, Yves could only make out a few words before his host saw him and nodded in greeting.

"Good morning, my friend Yves. I trust you slept well?"

"I did indeed, and thank you kindly for the comfortable accommodations."

"It is my pleasure to be of service to one who seeks to avoid the violence of warfare, and who further is assisting a fugitive from slavery."

Amalie came downstairs, more thoroughly dressed than Yves, but still informally garbed, with only an apron and a small cape fastened over her shift. She sat down, looking bleary-eyed, and stared out through the front window at the harbor.

Moses greeted her as well. "Good morning, Amalie. You look as though you were sleeping soundly when I sent Obidiah up to fetch you."

She nodded wordlessly and yawned. Moses called out to his wife, who brought in a teapot and a cup for Amalie. She set them down before the girl, and then poured her a cup. Amalie wrapped her hands around the cup and lifted it to her nose, inhaling appreciatively. She thanked her hostess, and then sipped from the tea as Mary returned to the kitchen.

Yves smiled at the girl's weariness and sympathized with her for so clearly wishing that she were still in bed.

Moses cleared his throat and said, "Amalie, I have some

things to discuss with you when you have had a chance to wake up further." She nodded and sipped from her tea again. Moses spoke to his daughter, and the girl rose and gracefully followed her mother into the kitchen. Both women emerged shortly, carrying the morning meal to the table. Mary called Moses' son in and he raced to his seat, making a show of being ravenous, and bringing laughter to those already seated.

After they'd had their fill, Amalie said softly, "I am ready to hear what plans you have for me now."

Moses looked up at her sharply. "Not plans, Amalie, but choices. Your fate is in your own hands, and you will need to make your own decisions as to how you will navigate the many paths open before you."

She nodded and he continued, "I've been talking over options for your long-term safety and security with Thomas, and have consulted some of my friends about the town already this morning. We see a number of paths for you."

He ticked them off on his fingers as he listed them. "You could stay here in Providence and find some employment here, whether as a domestic, or in some other useful trade that you may know. Thomas says that you have experience with stables; that is always in demand, particularly with the more affluent merchants and churchmen and so forth. Of course, though you would find friendly faces from this household to greet you on the street, you might also encounter slave catchers, checking to see if you'd come this far from Newport."

Moving to the next finger, he continued, "You could continue to Boston or even Philadelphia, where so many live that you could do likewise, with scarcely any fear of being recaptured, and live out your life in freedom and relative security. Of course, both are also targets of the English, and should the war go ill, they may re-occupy or even raze those cities in retribution for the losses imposed upon the Crown by the rebellion. Life could be strange and difficult for anyone there, let alone a free black woman."

"Finally, you could go to the frontier, where there are few people to ask difficult questions, and where no slave catcher is ever going to go looking for you. There is always the risk of military action overrunning your home there, and you must also be ready to contend with the Indians, who have on occasion conducted vicious raids and indulged in appalling violence against the settlers."

Yves spoke up, saying, "Have we not concluded an alliance with the Indians, so that they will direct their attentions only to the English?"

"We may have allied with a few of their tribes, but what you must understand is that they comprise dozens of nations, each of which has its own interests and needs. Most have chosen to remain neutral in this war, but many have taken up arms against anyone—patriot and Loyalist alike—whom they believe to have encroached on their lands, or to have taken their hunting. Sometimes they attack a settlement in retribution for the actions of a different settlement that has wronged them; I think that they must find our notions of community and nation as puzzling as we sometimes find theirs."

Yves nodded and Moses continued, now addressing him directly. "Your options are very similar, though I do not recommend staying here for very long, as the French are very often about town, and if they should move to join some other army contesting a field of battle, they will likely pass through here."

Yves shrugged in answer. "I'll have to learn English as well, in order to be of any use to anyone."

"You'll get by, I am sure." Moses glanced at Amalie. "Your friend learned the language under far worse conditions than you will."

Amalie spoke up now. "I am not accustomed to life in a large town, although I might well find employment on the outskirts of a town such as Providence. I enjoy caring for horses, but I suspect that for free servants, as for slaves, work in the house is better esteemed. The frontier sounds the safest, but I cannot readily imagine how I would make a living there."

She sighed. "How soon must I make a decision? I should like some time to think all of this over."

Moses smiled gently and reached across the table to pat the young woman's hand. "I am glad to offer you—all of you—a sanctuary here for as long as you need. Yves will probably need to stay indoors, though, to avoid the possibility of being recognized."

She said, "Thank you, again, for your generosity and assistance."

Their host waved his hand dismissively. "I have already told you that I am but attempting to relieve a burden that will never leave my soul."

As they talked, Yves frowned, thinking furiously. He felt sure that Amalie's best option was to be as far out of harm's way as possible, and he did not particularly like the idea of leaving her fate up to the fortunes of war.

Wherever she decided to go, he realized in a rush of discovery, he wanted to go with her, to keep her safe from all hazards. He glanced up at her and found that her gaze was locked onto him. She gave a tiny shrug, her eyes burning into his, and his decision was made.

He turned and faced Moses. "Amalie and I will go together to the frontier, and we will see what sort of life we can build together there."

Moses' eyebrows rose, but he did not make any comment at first. He looked at both of the two in turn, and Yves was only barely surprised to feel Amalie's hand steal into his own.

"You are certain about this?"

Yves knew that the man did not mean the choice of their destination, and he answered the question that was being asked. "I have but limited experience in this world . . . but I feel as certain about this as I have about anything in that experience."

Moses nodded slowly. Thomas looked on, his eyes narrowed in uncertainty. He asked a brief question, and Amalie answered him, her soft voice carrying a hint of steel within it. Yves squeezed her hand as she spoke and she returned the gesture.

After a moment of confusion registering on his face, he broke into an enormous smile, threw his hands up, and said something brief and clearly pleased with this plan of action.

Amalie turned to Moses and said, "Well, I am glad that is settled. I should like to speak with Yves alone for a little while, if we may. Can we use your sitting room?"

Moses smiled indulgently, waving them into the next room. "But of course."

Amalie led Yves into the great room, never releasing his hand. They sat together before the hearth, where the morning fire had been kindled, and offered a cheery accompaniment to their discussion.

She said softly, "I should like to understand how you mean

for us to live together. Will you employ me, or . . . ?"

Yves shook his head emphatically. "I shall never be your master, Amalie, in any way. We live as equals."

She nodded and said hesitantly, "I find that I feel for you a sense of friendship that goes beyond friendship, if you understand."

Yves looked up sharply and found her eyes steady and serene on his. She continued, "I do not know where this feeling leads, or even whether it can lead anywhere . . . but I want to follow it to find out, if you do."

"Are you so certain of your heart in just a handful of days?"

She smiled gently, shaking her head. "I have known ever since you told me that your life was forfeit if you were caught in trying to help me to escape to safety." She closed her eyes and took a deep breath. "I do not know if it is proper for someone such as myself to speak of it in regard to someone such as yourself, but I cannot deny that it was in that moment that I realized that I loved you."

Yves felt his heart suddenly lurch as the word crossed her lips, and the room seemed to spin for a moment. He closed his eyes and nodded slowly, willing his heart to stop racing, and the room to be still.

When he opened them, he saw her holding his hand, and he felt as though his thoughts were completely clear for the first time in his life. "Yes, I know. And . . . that is what I felt, too, when I decided to come with you. I have dared not speak of it. I know that my kind are supposed to hold ourselves as separate and different from yours, and I know that many will not find it proper to do otherwise."

He squeezed her hands gently for emphasis. "But we are not so different, in the things that matter. We both yearn for our freedom, and we both find comfort in a friendly smile. We fear the same things, and we bleed the same blood."

He shook his head. "If we love, if our hearts beat the same way, and our hands fit together, then how can we hold ourselves as hopelessly different, as not somehow having the same innate humanity?" He looked up and saw that her eyes were brimming with tears.

She wiped them away with her free hand and said only, "Yes. All of that, yes." Then she was in his arms, sobbing into his shoulder, and he was patting her back to comfort her.

Chapter 26

Yves and Amalie sat quietly side-by-side at the dinner table, listening to the conversation range up and down its length. Amalie translated the most interesting parts for Yves, as had become their habit over the past fortnight under Moses' roof.

Though Yves chafed to get out of town—he was tired of being confined to the four walls of the house, no matter how comfortable—the time had not been wasted. Moses had sent word to a few trusted friends and associates along the frontiers, seeking advice as to a likely-seeming destination for the young couple.

Though Yves had been braced for it, there had been no more than a raised eyebrow from the older Quakers in reaction to his calm announcement after breakfast on that fateful morning that he and Amalie had found love in each other's hearts.

Moses' teenaged daughter Sarah, though, had gasped in surprise at the match, saying something that Amalie refused to translate, but to which she responded in clipped words. Sarah had left the room abruptly when Moses had given her a grim, disapproving stare, and they had seen very little of her since the incident.

Obidiah, on the other hand, had shrugged and gone about his business when he came upon the couple standing close together, holding hands, and talking intently in the back hallway. Yves had blushed at being caught, but Amalie had smiled cheerily and patted his cheek.

At most of the meals since their arrival, the conversation had focused on practical, concrete questions of their future; the intangible was clearly accepted as a settled matter.

The question of their occupations had quickly winnowed down to a pretty narrow set of possibilities; outside of military pursuits, which held no ongoing charms for him, Yves' only other real experience was in farming. Fortunately, his father's farm had been a relatively generalized one, so he had experience in growing a wide range of crops.

Amalie, of course, knew horses, so if they could raise the capital, they could undertake horse breeding, and in the meantime, she could provide care for horses owned by neighbors. Thomas had said that he would like to accompany them, if they could suffer his presence, and he offered his knowledge of clearing and managing land on this side of the Atlantic.

Yves was only mildly surprised—the old gentleman had become a source of counsel to Amalie, and had cheerfully taken part in the ongoing process of assisting with Yves' slowly improving English—and Amalie had accepted his offer with a broad, grateful smile.

Tonight, though, the topic was the news that had hit the town like a thunderclap that morning—Benedict Arnold, the American general in charge of their most secure fortification at West Point, New-York, a leader who had an impressive record of success and sacrifice for the cause of the rebellion against England, had just been discovered to have gone over to the English side.

They dined tonight with a guest, a man whose name Yves forgot as soon as he heard it, but who had been learning what he could of the details of the betrayal and its discovery. Yves was doing his best to keep up with the torrent of English conversation, and was pleased to realize that he understood much of it even without Amalie's assistance.

"The plot was discovered when an English officer, a Major André, was captured and found to have been carrying in concealment a variety of documents conveying intelligence of the American fortifications, as well as detailed information about where their forces are, and their condition."

Yves put a hand to his chest in horror. "It is a—what is the word?—a *catastrophe* for the English to learn these informations! How was it trace to Arnold?"

"Shush, I am getting to that part. Apparently, the general got some word of André's capture, and immediately flew to the English ship that rested in the river below the fort, and which had been supposed to be there to gather intelligence in preparation for an attempt on the fort. I have heard that our men believe that the ship was there for the express purpose of providing passage to the English side for the traitor, as well as for carrying the English officers who participated in persuading him to turn his back on his nation."

Yves shook his head in disbelief that such treachery should have befallen the American cause. It reinforced his conviction that their rebellion was doomed. "It is a terrible day for the Americans."

"It is not so terrible as it might have been, though. Had the English been able to act as the traitor had intended, they would have taken not only the West Point fortifications and all of the soldiers within, but General Washington as well."

Yves gasped aloud. "They cannot capture the traitor and send him for hang to his actions?"

The other man frowned for a moment, puzzling through what Yves was trying to ask, before he answered, "No, it seems that the only object that we have for our anger is the unfortunate Major André, who has already been found guilty of espionage, it is said, and has been hanged as a spy, though he begged to be treated as an ordinary prisoner, in keeping with the rules of war."

Moses' guest finished his wine and stood, explaining, "I beg your pardon, and the indulgence of our host, but I have matters to which I must attend before the hour grows too late." He bowed to Moses, who nodded gravely to him.

As the man left, Amalie gave Yves a puzzled look and asked in French, "War has rules? What I have heard of war has always seemed to me to be a wholly uncivilized and lawless business, with men blasting away at one another, or worse, hacking each other to bits with their hangers and bayonets."

He shook his head, smiling. "Oh, no, there are many rules and customary usages of wartime. For example, a man who approaches under a white flag is considered to be on a mission of peace, whether to parley or to ask for a merciful stop to fighting, to permit both sides to recover their dead and tend to their wounded."

He frowned. "I am not as clear as to the customs or rules of determining the difference between espionage and mere observation of the enemy's movements and positions, but I trust that those who sat in judgment of the English officer were well acquainted with those rules, and applied them with the same fairness that they would like to see applied to one of their own officers under similar circumstances in the hands of the English."

Yves shrugged, concluding, "It all comes down to that, in the end: you treat the enemy as you would like to be treated, and trust that he will do likewise. If that covenant is broken, warfare devolves into the sort of savagery that you described, and none may hope to exit the field of battle in honor or safety, regardless of the outcome."

She shuddered and squeezed his hand. "I am glad that you are done with that business, in any event. I could not bear the thought of you presenting yourself to any such hazards, regardless of the cause."

He smiled grimly. "If it should come down to a matter of protecting you, I should gladly take up arms again, but no king or Congress will compel me to do so for reasons which are not my own."

Moses looked up at this comment and interjected, "I would like to be enough of a peaceable influence upon you that you might find some other path than violence, even if you or Amalie are threatened."

"I have not your experience of the world, Moses, but if an English regiment or slave catcher or even just ordinary ruffians should fall upon us, I could see little alternative to meeting violence with violence."

Moses grimaced. "I wish I had the time to argue the finer points of theology with you, my young friend, but I will say this much: there is always another way than violence, even when we are met with violence ourselves. It may be more difficult, and it may be more uncomfortable, but the light commands us to seek it wherever possible."

"I can make you no promises, where Amalie's safety is

concerned,"—he squeezed her hand under the table, and she returned the gesture—"but I will do my best to look for alternatives when they are possible."

Moses sat back, nodding. "No more can I ask of you. I only hope that it never becomes necessary for you to face that choice."

"As do I." In his heart, though, Yves wondered whether two fugitives in a time of war could ever avoid having to make the choice between violence and extinction.

Chapter 27

Yves and Amalie were in the sitting room, just enjoying the fire and each other's company after a storm-swept night had kept them both awake late into the evening, when Moses came in and asked, "May I join you for a few minutes?"

Amalie tilted her head curiously and said, "It is your sitting room—you may do as you wish in it."

Moses smiled and took a seat facing the young couple. He began without preamble, "I know that one of the problems you have been wrestling with is how to find a place where you can acquire the land you need."

He sighed. "While it is true that one can simply occupy a tract of land on the Pennsylvania frontier, and that there are provisions in the laws of that state to convert your possession of the tract into a legitimate ownership, your status adds further, unnecessary complications to that process."

Yves nodded, grimacing. He had already had this discussion with Thomas, who still favored this approach over the alternatives.

"Of course, if you had money, or the prospect of earning a substantial amount over what you need to support yourselves, you could probably make an arrangement to purchase a land patent, either outright, or at terms that you could somehow afford."

Yves interjected, "We could also enter into a tenancy on

land that someone else owned the grant for, but was unable to work himself, for whatever reason." This was the option that Yves himself preferred, though Amalie wanted very much to be free of any hint of an outside master, even one who was called more gently a landlord.

Moses nodded. "That is a good alternative for young people just starting out, but it leaves you without permanency. Well," he said, lifting his eyes heavenward, "what permanency this world of turmoil can offer. In any event, I hope that you don't mind that I have taken the liberty of attempting to resolve that problem on your behalf."

He drew from his pocket a folded sheet of paper, which he held out to Yves. Yves accepted it, his hands trembling with sudden apprehension. He unfolded it to find densely-written, fine script, all in English, accompanied by a labeled drawing that looked like a diagonal square, with a forked line running through it.

He offered it to Amalie, who glanced at it and said sadly, "I cannot read."

"And I can only read a little bit, and that in French," Yves added, holding the paper back out to Moses.

"Ah," the older man said, and accepted the paper. "Then I shall read it for you."

Moses took a deep breath and read in a rapid monotone, "To all to whom these presents shall come, greeting: Know ye that in consideration for one dollar in hand and other valuable services and considerations, there is conveyed to Yves de Bourganes a certain tract or parcel of land containing sixty acres by survey bearing date the seventh day of the sixth month in the year of one thousand seven hundred and seventy-nine, situated and being in the county of Hartford, in Connecticut State, and butted and bounded as follows, namely: to the east by a highway that runs through the common field; to the north by land belonging to the heirs of Jebidiah Greene, deceased; to the west by land belonging to Nathaniel Waterhouse; and to the south by land belonging to Moses Brown who resides in Providence, Rhode-Island, through which runs a branch of the Pequabuck River, which forms a pond thereon; together with the privileges and thereof thereon or thereto belonging, to have and to the named conveyed premises with all the dependencies to the named Yves de Bourganes, his heirs, and assigns forever. Executed under my hand by the named Moses Brown, on the tenth day of the tenth month in the year of one thousand seven hundred and eighty."

He folded the paper back up and handed it to Yves again, who accepted it with a now visibly shaking hand. "I have extensive land holdings, and as I considered various places where you might go, this one came to mind. It is undeveloped, and the community there is dominated by Congregationalists, though there had been an active Episcopal Church there as well, and a fair concentration of Loyalists. I am told"—his mouth twitched as he suppressed a smile—"that those whose loyalties laid with the English King have been persuaded to declare for the rebels, or else depart. What Indians are present there have a reputation for friendly relations with the settlers in their midst, and for abiding by the agreements they have made with the white men. In short, it is a quiet place, and one where you can pursue your lives in peace. What say you?"

Yves was at a loss for words, and he could feel Amalie stunned into silence beside him. He finally spoke, his voice quavering slightly. "I already owe a debt to Benjamin, back in Newport, who showed us forbearance beyond all reason, and through whom we came to know Thomas. I have promised to repay that debt by showing equal kindness and hospitality to someone in need. This . . . this I could never repay in this life."

Moses smiled gently at the couple. "The land must, by law, be titled in your name, but the debt to repay is mine, to Amalie, for the crimes committed against the slaves who were taken and mistreated to their deaths, in my name. As I have related to you previously, I cannot ever unmake those mistakes of my youth; all that I can do is to right the wrongs committed now against others, wherever it is in my power to do so. This is well within my power to do, and I sincerely hope that you will accept it, and enable me to pay some of *my* debt."

Amalie sat up in her chair as Moses spoke, wonder and understanding spreading over her face. "We will accept your boon, Moses, though I know that we will still feel the obligation to do what is in our power to do the sort of good work that you now do." She rose from her seat and embraced the older man, which seemed to take him by surprise, based on the awkwardness with which he returned the embrace.

Yves stood and embraced Moses in turn, as soon as Amalie released him, still struck speechless, and still shaking in disbelief.

All three resumed their seats, and when Yves had regained the power of speech, he said simply, "Thank you. I . . . I cannot add any words to this. Thank you."

Moses nodded solemnly. "Now that that is settled, there is another matter which I must discuss with you. I know not whether it will have any bearing on your future, but I ask only that you hear me out." He stopped and looked at both of them expectantly.

Confused, both Amalie and Yves nodded, and Yves said, "Do go on."

Moses said, "Very well. I have taken the further liberty of acquainting myself with the laws that pertain to marriage in the different parts of this new nation."

Yves looked sharply at Amalie, and then back to Moses, a deep blush spreading over his features. "We have not dis—"

Moses held up a hand, interrupting him. "Hear me out; as I said, I know not whether this pertains to any plans that you may have laid, or may even consider in the future, but I wanted you to be armed with the knowledge before you begin making any decisions, in one direction or another."

Yves nodded slowly, still flushed nearly brick-red. Amalie, for her part, seemed hardly to be breathing, and her eyes bored into Moses' as the older man continued.

"As you may already know, some states in this country bar marriage between the races. Pennsylvania had done so, but this spring repealed that state's ban for free blacks. Connecticut has never had a law on the matter, which may, at some point in the future, turn out to be a useful thing to know about the state where you now own a homestead. There, I will say no more on that matter, but consider my duty to you in this regard as having been wholly discharged."

Yves felt the blush slowly fading, and he said, as evenly as he could, "Thank you again, Moses, for the information."

"It is my pleasure, again, to have shared it with you. I wish you both nothing but the best, and whatever form it may take, a long and happy life together. I presume that you may be eager to depart for your new home, and I have made the necessary arrangements.

Thomas awaits with a wagon of a few necessities, and a pair of promising horses, which I trust you can manage, Amalie."

The girl had remained stoic in her joy up to this point, but now she burst into tears, to everyone's surprise including her own. She protested, "You are too kind!"

Moses said sternly, "No, if I were too kind, I would never have participated in the voyage of the *Sally* in any capacity. What I am is deeply aware of what you have suffered under the wicked institution that I once participated in."

He made a decisive gesture. "I have said already that I am glad for the opportunity that I have had to compensate you in some small measure for the years of your life and labor that were stolen from you."

Standing, he said, "I shall gather the household to bid you farewell, and a safe and rapid passage to Connecticut."

Chapter 28

Thomas drove the wagon, while Amalie and Yves walked alongside, through a deeply-shaded woodland road. The wagon was well-worn, but generously loaded with building materials and household goods, and drawn by a pair of truly magnificent horses, as Moses had understated the magnitude of his final gift to Amalie.

Yves was filled with wonder at the riot of colors that the trees contrived to produce in their autumnal leaves, and felt that the rich scent of the warm fall air might well be the most lovely thing he had ever smelled. His heart was likewise filled with warmth and leapt with joy every time he saw Amalie glance over at him and smile.

The road to Connecticut had been uncertain at some points, and while Moses had asked them to stay at taverns and inns whenever they could, they had been forced to sleep under the wagon a few times. The weather, though, had been gentle, having apparently expended its fury in the nights before their departure, and they had experienced no adverse encounters.

The sweet, light breezes carried birdsong and the occasional chittering scream of a squirrel offended by their passage through its territory.

They rounded a bend, and Thomas called out, "I see a pond—I think that this may be it!"

Amalie and Yves hurried to the front of the wagon, and stopped alongside their friend. Together, they looked out over a lightly-wooded land, bordering a long, narrow pond with a gentle, rocky beach on one side. Yves felt Amalie's hand slip into his own and he smiled at her, his heart content. His path had led him home.

Historical
Notes

When Rochambeau sailed from France to America, it was, just as depicted in the pages of this book, an exceptionally eventful period in the history of the young nation. Not only would Rochambeau's force join up with Washington's the following year at Yorktown, bringing about the decisive final battle of the American Revolution, but we also suffered our most terrible betrayal of the war, at the hands of a disgruntled young general who felt that he had been persecuted and maltreated by General Washington and the Congress.

The events of the voyage from France to Rhode-Island are well documented, and I have depicted them with as much fidelity as I could. Likewise, the visit of the Haudenosaunee (Iroquois) delegation to the French encampment at Newport was, as depicted, an excuse for both the French and the Indians to show off a bit for one another. Sharp-eyed readers will note the return of a familiar name in that party of Haudenosaunee, a man who has had a few years to recover since the last time we saw him in the pages of *The Smoke*.

I have placed Yves loosely in a company of *chausseurs*—infantrymen—in Lauzon's Regiment, which was attached to Rochambeau's *Expédition Particulière*, bound for America. Lauzon's Regiment was initially slated to participate in a direct invasion of the English homeland, but when that plan was scrubbed, he accompanied Rochambeau to America. There, his units were noted for their lax conduct, frequent brawls and duels, and a certain degree of separation from the movements and practices of the rest of Rochambeau's forces.

In fact, Lauzon's Regiment was encamped entirely separate from the main force of Rochambeau's expedition, according to a contemporaneous map; for dramatic purposes, I have placed Yves' company within the primary encampment, closer to the village.

The conditions of the town of Newport, as I described them, are supported by multiple sources, including the detail that would likely have been of the most interest to young, virile French soldiers that some three-quarters of the remaining residents were female.

Sadly, the circumstances of the slaves of Rhode-Island was also remarked upon by the Frenchmen who kept journals of their impressions of their travels through America. Slavery, although rarer than in the Southern colonies, persisted in Rhode-Island until about 1840, following the passage of emancipation legislation in 1784. (The legislation only applied to slaves born after 1 March 1784, and only freed them when they reached the age of 18 and 21, respectively, for girls and boys born into slavery.)

Rhode Island's merchants were among the primary importers of slaves, but the overwhelming majority of their tragic stock was sold in the Caribbean or the Southern colonies of the prewar British American holdings. The slave trade to the nascent United States was pretty well stopped during the course of the war, due to blockades and the threat of prize-seeking English ships.

The purchase of horses for the French company of Hussars was mentioned in passing, but the character of the horse seller, and his slave, are inventions of my own imagination. The existence of an early version of an underground railroad for escaped slaves, centered around the members of the Society of Friends ("Quakers") is factual, though, which brings us to one of the most fascinating characters we encountered in the pages of this book.

Moses Brown was an historical figure, and he is interwoven through the early history of the state of Rhode-Island. Not only was he actually one of the brothers who was involved in underwriting the slave mission that turned into the Sally disaster, but he also did go on to join the Society of Friends, and became a prominent abolitionist around the time of the Revolution.

I have surmised that his reasons for doing so stemmed from the guilt that he felt about his involvement in the *Sally*, but I do not have any firm evidence at this time to support that supposition. We do know that he never again supported the involvement of the family business in slavery, and he freed his own slaves in 1773, nearly a decade before the events of this novel.

I do not have any documentation of what languages Moses Brown spoke, but it seemed reasonable to me that he would have learned French as a matter of business efficiency, as Quaker merchants were frequently accused of using their opposition to warfare as a convenient excuse to do business with all sides, and there are some accusations that the Brown brothers were involved in trade with the French during the Seven Years' War, known in North America as the French and Indian War.

His brother John was considered the ringleader of the attack on the British customs ship the *Gaspee*, and Moses Brown was one of the leaders of the efforts to secure his brother's release, and to oppose him being shipped back to England for trial and (presumably) execution.

The incident with the *Gaspee* represents the unacknowledged beginning of the formal hostilities between the American colonies and Mother Britain—in any age, firing upon a seagoing vessel of a government is considered to be an unambiguous act of war.

Later, the apparently unrepentant John Brown was the first man to be tried for violating the Federal Slave Trade Act of 1794. (He was acquitted, due to his power and wealth, but his ship, the ironically-named *Hope*, was confiscated a year later for continued violations.)

Moses Brown was quite prosperous, and did have extensive land holdings around New England, so it seemed at least plausible to me that he would have made use of those resources to help an escaped slave and deserted French soldier as I've depicted.

Mary was his second wife of three—he outlived them all, as well as all of his own children, and three of his four step-children. Before he died at the age of 98, he participated in initiating the Industrial Revolution in the United States, founding a textile mill that operated on a water wheel. He and his brothers helped to found Brown University, as well as today's Moses Brown School.

Moses Brown was an amazingly influential figure in the history of the Colonial, Revolutionary, and Early Republic periods of American history, and I am surprised that he is not better represented in fiction. I hope that my affectionate depiction of him helps to correct this injustice to some degree, and that I have not erred too widely in my characterization of this truly complex and fascinating man.

As an aside, my depiction of his daughter's reaction to Yves and Amalie's budding relationship is not in any way supported by information that I have about her as an individual, and was meant only to represent the opposition that they would experience all their lives.

A brief note about the language: as I depicted the Quaker characters either translated by Amalie or speaking French themselves, I did not emphasize the "thee-thou" mode of their "plain speech" when I rendered them into English for the purposes of this narrative. If you would like to experience a full rendition of Quaker plain speech, it's very carefully and faithfully represented in my novel *The Light*.

Acknowledgements

Trying to tell the familiar story of the American uprising from the point of view of an outsider sent to take part was a daunting challenge, but a number of indespensible resources gave me some hints from which I could work. The journal of Baron von Closen, who traveled with the *Expédition Particulière*, was particularly valuable in understanding the trials and tribulations of the voyage to America from France, and offered insights as to how America appeared in the eyes of our French guests.

On the less savory side, the important and detailed timeline of the terrible voyage of the Sally maintained by the library at Brown University was a sobering reminder of the uglier side of New-England commerce in the years leading up to the Revolution.

Christian McBurney of Small State Big History offered invaluable suggestions regarding several of the historical details included in The Path, and Craig Alarie of Le Regiment Bourbonnais provided important details of the French experience in Rhode Island.

My editor, Ingrid Bevz of Green Ink Proofreading (who will probably frown at my use of commas here), helped me to greatly improve several key passages, as well as providing the gentle prod of necessary corrections for typos and grammatical errors, plus the inevitable abuse of my comma key.

Errors, omissions, and oversights remain as always, my own.

Thank You

I deeply appreciate you spending the past couple of hundred pages with the characters and events of a world long past, yet hopefully relevant today.

If you enjoyed this book, I'd also be grateful for a kind review on your favorite bookseller's Web site or social media outlet. Word of mouth is the best way to make me successful, so that I can bring you even more high-quality stories of bygone times.

I'd love to hear directly from you, too—feel free to reach out to me via my Facebook page, Twitter feed, or Web site and let me know what you liked, and what you would like me to work on more.

Again, thank you for reading, for telling your friends about this book, for giving it as a gift or dropping off a copy in your favorite classroom or library. With your support and encouragement, we'll find even more times and places to explore together.

larsdhhedbor.com
Facebook: LarsDHHedbor
@LarsDHHedbor on Twitter

Enjoy a preview of the next book in the
Tales From a Revolution series:

The Free

It was all over now. Calabar recognized the final rattle of breath from sitting by his own mother's deathbed, and he knew that his master's days were done.

Frederick Greene would never again rise from the mattress he had ordered Calabar to stuff with fresh straw earlier in the summer. The slave stood, reaching up to knead the tension out of his own shoulder, and methodically thinking through what must be done next.

Mister Greene's son, a busy and prosperous tobacco farmer, must be summoned. Calabar felt the first stab of panic at that thought, as he did not trust what the younger Greene might decide to do with him, Affey, and their newborn daughter. He suppressed his fear, though, to focus on what must be done.

He ducked through the doorway of his master's bedroom, stepped out through the kitchen door and called out, "Affey! Come and help me saddle up Mister Greene's horse."

Affey appeared around the corner of the house, worry and fear written across her broad face. The baby was swaddled as usual in a sling against her chest, and she instinctively pulled her closer as she said in a quavering voice, "Is he...?"

Calabar nodded solemnly. "I need to go and bring word to Master Greene. We must be ready to help him with whatever arrangements he will make for his father."

He grimaced, adding, "Master Greene... owns us now."

Affey's tears started in earnest now, though Calabar knew from the swirl of emotions that rampaged through his own heart that she wept not so much for their departed master as for the potential chaos that his death was sure to bring in its wake.

Calabar stepped forward and pulled her into his arms, but only for a moment. "We must be strong now, Affey. We cannot control what happens after this. We can only do what must be done. Right now, I need to ride that horse."

Affey nodded, wiping her tears away. She followed him to the stable and led the old mare out of her stall to blink lazily in the bright summer sunlight. Calabar was ready with the saddle, swinging it up onto the horse's back, and Affey wordlessly reached under the animal's belly to pass him the cinch.

He grunted in thanks and secured it, pulling it tight and waiting for the mare to exhale, before tightening it completely. He remembered the only time he'd fallen for the horse's trick ruefully, and remembered, too, the harsh words Mister Greene had lavished on him.

The master had returned, half an hour after the mare had ambled in, and Calabar was thankful that the man had had the long walk home to calm down a bit. If it had happened closer by, Calabar was reasonably sure that Mister Greene would have whipped him for his mistake.

As it was, his master had required Calabar to sweep and scrub the entirety of the stable until it gleamed, giving the slave no rest until the job was done. Calabar remembered few nights when he had been as grateful to fall into his bed of straw as that one, and even the full moon – high in the sky by the time he'd finished the job – could not keep him awake.

Shaking his head to dismiss the memory, Calabar slipped the bridle over the horse's head and slipped the bit between her teeth. He placed his foot into the stirrup as he'd seen Mister Greene do so many times, and attempted to swing himself up onto her back. He succeeded only in kicking her in the hindquarters, and she shied away, giving him a baleful glance over her shoulder.

Affey was struggling to keep a smile off her face, her lips pressed together in firm and serious determination, though her eyes told a wholly different story. Calabar sighed and said, "Fetch me that stool, if you could."

Stepping up onto the short stool, he tried again, and succeeded in getting himself up onto the saddle, albeit without his legs straddling the animal. Gracelessly, he scrambled into a seated position and worked his other foot into the stirrup.

Affey looked up at him. "Are you sure you should ride, and not just walk?"

He sighed, picking the reins up as he'd seen Mister Greene do on many occasions. "I may wind up walking. I should try to get there quick as I can, though."

He pulled the reins to one side, urging the horse to turn. She bent her neck in the direction he was pulling, but did not move her feet at all. He pulled harder, and the horse tossed her head and then started back for her stable, carrying Calabar along on her back helplessly.

Affey followed, her expression no longer concealing mirth, but instead sharing in Calabar's obvious frustration. "Should I lead her back out?"

He shook his head in resignation. "I will just walk," he said, pulling his foot out of the stirrup and swinging it over the mare's back to jump down. "Can you remove the tack?" He got his other foot free of its stirrup and slid down to the ground.

She nodded, and bent to start loosening the saddle, protecting the baby's head with one hand as she did so.

"Thank you, Affey. I had best set out. I will make up what time I can." He sighed again, grimacing. "I'll tell Shampee on my way. He will gather the others."

With no more than a quick glance back, Calabar set out down the road from the big house, between the fields grown waist-high on both sides of the road with the bushy indigo plants that had made Mister Greene so prosperous in life.

As he ran, he could hear the scream of a locust and smelled the damp earth of the fields. He breathed in deeply, glad that it was not yet harvest season – once the slaves began processing the indigo, the reek of the fermenting leaves would overpower everything else as far as the eye could see.

He approached the three-tiered processing vats and found Shampee, the plantation's slave driver, fetching water to bring to the crew working the field beyond the structure. He slowed to a walk, mastering his breath so that he could speak to the other slave.

Shampee looked up at Calabar's approach, concern clear in his expression. Mister Greene had been ill since the prior evening, and his condition had been a topic of conversation and speculation in the slave quarters far past the setting of the sun.

Calabar nodded in greeting to Shampee and said simply, "Mister Greene is dead. I'm going to go tell Master Greene. He will need to make arrangements."

Shampee's mouth fell open, and he said, slowly shaking his head, "Thought for sure that he was gonna pull through." His gravelly voice concealed any grief he was feeling, but he grimaced, betraying his emotions. "And just before the harvest, too."

Looking around at the indigo in the fields, Calabar agreed, "It's going to be a good crop, too. Shame Mister Greene didn't see it come in."

He motioned with his head back up the road. "I had best be off, Shampee. You gather the others and wait for Master Greene."

Shampee nodded. "Gonna be some changes here." He grimaced again, and turned toward the fields, his steps mechanical.

Look for The Free: Tales From a Revolution - North-Carolina *at your favorite booksellers.*

the text works. We lack precise remarks about structure, the 'self-conscious' aspects of the composition beyond the basic idea of the *composition en abyme,* or its deliberate artificiality. Also, whereas Gide's theoretical ambitions are usually presented by him singly, when they are realized in the text they relate to each other in ways that are themselves highly significant. The text has, furthermore, to be seen as the product of a constant process of relativization, establishing its truths in the manner of a dialectic and at every level constructed with the aid of a skilful manipulation of paradox.

Equally, many of the ideas Gide does parade, such as that of the *roman pur,* receive from him a highly general, not to say vague, formulation. For it was only through his practice that he was able to establish his true and often subtle position with regard to these ideas. So, if we confine ourselves to his own criteria, we remain in the realm of half-truths, simplifying this complex work and conveniently ignoring its teasing paradoxes. Yet when all is said and done, much of the value of analysing this novel comes as a result of discovering that what we thought was simple is complex and that what we thought was the whole truth is only partially applicable. In this chapter, therefore, I shall be attempting to show both the extent to which *Les Faux-Monnayeurs* actualizes the experimental ambitions expressed by Gide and Edouard, and the fact that many of the most crucial features of the text are in their discussions left unexplained.

There is, I think, a good case to be made for concluding that Gide has largely been successful in creating an impression of inclusiveness, and in such a way that an impression of naturalness is produced at the same time. Nearly all the events touch upon Edouard's life (aged 36, he is situated half way between the old and the young) and as a result the reader has the feeling that the account of his life in this period is more or less complete. The presentation of these events is, moreover, made much more lifelike by virtue of their being freed from the constraints of a conventional novelistic plot. Gide is indeed closer than was the naturalist novel to capturing the way we naturally experience the individuals and events that surround us. The action is non-sequential, broken up realistically into a host of linked but none the less separate adventures (thereby partially realizing the ambition of Jacques Rivière and other members of the *NRF* group for a modern *roman d'aventures*). [1] For all the characters life is experienced as a continual present or, rather, a succession of present moments. The simultaneity of events is further emphasized by Gide's technique of suspending a character's adventure in mid-air, as it were, and passing on to a succession of other individual adventures that are likewise interrupted and temporarily lost from sight.

Another tactic successfully employed by Gide in his quest for naturalness is that of making the narrative style of both the narrator and Edouard for the most part quite unexceptional. Although the Gidean narrator is, on occasion, blatantly 'self-conscious', and although in his narrative events will sometimes appear contrived and indeed far-fetched, his descriptive manner, like that of Edouard, more usually contrasts with the widespread tendency of novelists to exhibit uncommon powers of observation and indulge in formal descriptions that, paradoxically, may have the opposite effect of 'realism', behaving as they do according to the dictates of conventional literary practice. The narrative styles of Gide's novel are indeed characterized by a spontaneity and ordinariness that for much of the time make their narrators appear in this respect little different from any of us when we comment upon and analyze what is going on around us. (If the reader of *Les Faux-Monnayeurs* is rarely able to forget he is reading a novel, it is always for other reasons.) There is, it will be noted, a marked lack of physical description of character or place. In other words, the presentation is, in one important sense, un-literary, a quality for which Gide consciously strove: 'le style des *Faux-Monnayeurs* ne doit présenter aucun intérêt de surface, aucune saillie' (*1*, p. 72).

As for Gide's desire for open-endedness, a satisfying impression of such a state is created on more than one level. ' "Pour-

---

[1] See Kevin O'Neill, *André Gide and the 'Roman d'Aventure'* (Sydney, Sydney U.P., 1969).

rait être continué..." c'est sur ces mots que je voudrais terminer mes *Faux-Monnayeurs*', says Edouard (p. 322). Gide's own choice of ending — Edouard expressing his desire to get to know young Caloub — is his way of reminding the reader that life goes on. The novel has indeed become known for its final sentence in the way that *Du Côté de chez Swann* and many other novels are known for the lines with which they open. (A perspicacious critic, Goulet, has noted, incidentally, that Caloub is an anagram of *boucla*! Gide wrote of his novel: 'Il ne doit pas se boucler, mais s'éparpiller, se défaire' (*1*, p. 84).) A more radical representation of the open-endedness of experience, though, is seen in Gide's depiction of character. It is frequently emphasized in this novel that character is a highly unstable entity. In the case of both Edouard and Gide, this realization leads to a state approaching a crisis of self. As Edouard says: 'Je ne suis jamais que ce que je crois que je suis — et cela varie sans cesse' (pp. 72-73). In his novel, Edouard will concern himself only with 'les possibilités de chaque être'. Gide's practice shows this to have been his ambition as well. One of his most considerable achievements in *Les Faux-Monnayeurs* is to have given the impression that many of his characters are free to behave in a number of different ways. (Where this is not the case, there is deliberate use of caricature for satirical effect.) One of his earliest readers, Crémieux, was quick to grasp our author's originality in this respect:

> La grande nouveauté psychologique qui vient sans cesse se mettre au travers du romancier, c'est désormais que l'acte n'est plus tout, que la souveraineté de l'acte est décidément déchue au point de vue de l'expression et de la connaissance intime de l'homme. Rien ne nous paraît plus d'un aussi mince intérêt que ces romans où un acte commis par hasard et faisant boule de neige entraîne le héros aux pires déchéances ou aux plus surprenantes réussites (*6*, p. 91).

But even more than this freedom from a series of related dramatic actions, it is Gide's representation of the *elusiveness* of character that warrants our attention.

The example of Laura may be found helpful. No two individuals view her in the same way. Each conception of her character is shaped by the role she plays in the life of that particular
observer. Yet it is not simply a matter of the observer's inev-
itably subjective and partial point of view: Gide rightly shows
that in part we act according to the role we think others expect
of us. If by the end of the novel the reader is slightly perplexed
by the different pictures he has received of Laura and feels he
has not really got to know her, this does not illustrate incon-
sistency in Gide's art of characterization but a deliberate avoid-
ance by him of a single, privileged viewpoint. Like all human
beings, Laura will in some ways remain hidden from both
herself and others. Further consideration of individual characters would reveal significant areas of uncertainty, and it is
no surprise that those who inhabit the world of *Les Faux-Monnayeurs* are frequently unhappy with the way they are viewed
by others.

The extent to which Gide is successful in making his characters appear to act independently of their author is, however,
open to debate. On several occasions, the authorial voice de-
clares either that it is ignorant of the actions of a character
or that it is surprised or disappointed by their behaviour. In
particular, the narrator's remarks in the final chapter of the
Saas-Fée section are meant to imply that his characters possess
a very high degree of autonomy. From one point of view such
a claim is patently absurd. The characters are the author's
creation and he can obviously make them behave as he thinks
fit. Seen in this light, the protestations of ignorance — 'J'aurais
été curieux de savoir ce qu'Antoine a pu raconter à son amie
la cuisinière; mais on ne peut tout écouter' (p. 30) — may appear so much coquetry. And there is no doubt they are to be
seen as contributing to the deliberately 'self-conscious' dimen-
sion of the novel. But they are perhaps not to be categorized
in so neat a fashion. It is, after all, true that the author is not
free to treat his characters in a cavalier fashion; a display of
omniscience would run counter to the impression of spontaneity
and naturalness that forms a large part of the novel's *raison
d'être*. Indeed, whatever reservations we have subsequently, it